THE SECRETS OF MYSTIC SPRINGS

A MYSTIC SPRINGS PARANORMAL COZY
MYSTERY

MONA MARPLE

This book is dedicated to two of my wonderful readers; Erik and Lou.

Thank you for supporting me.

As an author, I rely on the help of readers to spot those pesky typos that sneak through on each book. Thank you to Nadine Peterse-Vrijhof and Susan Coletta for your help tracking them down in this book!

1

SAGE

𝒥'm not sure how I ever had time to be alive. I'm too darn popular.

The problem with the whole of Mystic Springs being able to see us spirits is that everyone wants to talk to me.

I mean, I don't blame them. I'd want to be friends with me too, if I was them.

But it's so time consuming.

Not to mention how hard it makes it to spy on people, which has pretty much been my main hobby for the last twenty years. That and annoying Connie, of course.

Now, my days are filled with inane conversation - something I've really forgotten how to take part in. You have to give us spirits credit where it's due, we don't get bogged down with small talk.

You know, just two days ago, I was in the grocery store and I overheard two old women discuss potatoes for five minutes. Potatoes! I had to really try hard not to interrupt them and tell them to look in the mirror, check their wrinkles, and realise they didn't have time for that utter rubbish.

Potatoes.

Geeze.

There are good bits to this new way of life, though.

Connie looks less crazy when she sits and talks to spirits now, since everyone in town can see who she's talking to.

And she - bizarrely - has more time. I have less time and she has more. Go figure.

There's less call for her medium skills now everyone in town can see the spirits. Although other people can't tune in and request a special appearance by their favourite ghost, and only people in Mystic Springs can see the spirits, so there's still enough demand to keep her in the somewhat dull lifestyle she's grown accustomed to. She just has more time to relax, and more time to spend with me if I can fit her in my busy schedule.

It's like we're teenagers again, her trying to pin me down.

Let me tell you, it's pretty good to remember what it feels like to be popular. These last two decades of isolation have been pretty rough on the former Great Beauty of the Class of... well, I don't think we need to specify the year, do we?

Oh, and if you're still wondering how I died. I don't know! No, I haven't magically remembered. Stop being so gruesome, okay?

"Sage?" Connie says, which is bad news. She's sat across from me in the Screamin' Beans Coffee House and she's been blabbering on for at last three minutes about a programme she watched last night on the History channel. I've been trying to drown her out without her noticing.

"Is that right?" I say. If you ever find yourself in this situation, you've been caught, so you've got nothing to lose. You might as well give one last attempt at convincing the dull person that you were paying attention.

"You were listening?" Connie asks. Result!

"Of course I was." I say.

She glances down and now she's feeling guilty as Hell. I'm really too good at this. "You seemed miles away."

"I was just thinking." I say. "It sounds really interesting. Shame I missed it."

It absolutely was not a shame I missed it. I was out - with Patton Davey. On a real date. Well, a walk around town with no physical touching but a fair amount of flirting on my part. I'm claiming it.

"The second part's on tonight, let's watch it together." Connie suggests.

darn it! I really am too good at this.

"You know, I think I have..." I begin, but it's like looking at a puppy dog. The woman desperately needs some more Sage in her life. Who am I to say no? "I think I'm free."

"Really?" She asks, as astounded as I am that I'm agreeing to this.

"Uh huh." I say. "What's the second part called? I might look it up online."

"Oh, it's just part two. Wonders of the Egyptians." Connie says with a grin. "It's about Cleopatra. I've always loved her. Do you remember learning about her at school?"

"Vaguely." I admit. I quite enjoyed learning about the ancient Egyptians at school, although I was too cool to admit that, while Connie made no secret of her own enthusiasm. She sat up front at every class, taking notes and asking questions and turning herself into more of an outcast than she already was. I can handle a programme about this.

"I loved imagining that I was alive in those times." Connie says, all dreamy.

"Why?" I ask, and I crinkle my nose as I speak. She takes a sip from the huge mug of cocoa in front of her. "Life was so hard back then."

"Well, yeah, but they were also so advanced. So many of

the things we think are our modern inventions, they'd worked out first."

"Maybe you can channel Cleopatra's ghost." I say.

"Spirit." Connie corrects.

"Cleopatra's spirit..."

"Ooh!" Connie says, and she giggles. "Wouldn't that be amazing."

"It would give Atticus some new PR material." I say. Atticus, the former mayor, hasn't allowed a trifling detail like his death to stop his mission to put Mystic Springs firmly on the map.

"What's Atticus up to now?" Ellie, the coffee house owner, asks as she clears empty cups from the table next to us. She gives me a nervous smile but firmly directs the question to Connie.

"Oh, nothing. We're just talking about Cleopatra."

"Who?"

"Cleopatra, you know, from Ancient Egypt."

"Oh, I'm not really very up on history." Ellie says. "You need to talk to that guy about it, he's always banging on about old stuff."

I look across the room, to a table where a man in a light grey hoodie and a dark grey beret, vintage round glasses with dark frames, and a neat grey goatee sits across from a woman in a fur coat.

"He's a historian, that'll be why." Connie says, following my gaze. I've seen the man around town but can't name him, and now I know why. He must move in different circles to me. You know, the boring ones.

"A what?"

"A historian." Connie repeats. "You know, he studies the past, collects antiques and things."

"Oh." Ellie says, unimpressed. She has a tray full of

empty cups and she walks away, back towards the counter, balancing it in her arms.

"She's not an intellectual, like us." I joke.

Connie rolls her eyes. "She's a sweet girl."

"I never said she wasn't!" I protest. I actually like Ellie Bean a fair amount, if only because she has the ovaries to own the world's ugliest cat. Godiva sits on the floor near the counter, eyeing me as if reading my mind. Nasty animal.

"So what are your plans for the day? Until our hot date with Cleopatra, of course." I ask.

Connie's dressed in what is basically a tent, so I hope she's either going emergency clothes shopping or returning home to get changed.

"I've got some errands to run."

"Clothes shop kind of errands?" I ask, hopefully.

"Erm, no." Connie says. She looks down at the polka dot monstrosity. "Why, what's wrong with this? I thought these baggy dresses were in fashion."

"Really, baggy dresses flatter nobody over a size 10. I keep telling you to wear more fitted clothes."

"Fitted clothes will show off my wobbly bits." Connie says with a nervous laugh. She's been unhappy with her body for years, just not unhappy enough to put the biscuits down. Kind of like me every time I get my heart broken, just not quite broken enough to take a vow of abstinence from men.

"We've had this talk a million times. They might show off some wobbly bits but they'll still be more flattering than that tent."

The colour drains from Connie's face and I worry that I've pushed her too far, but then I realise she's looking behind me, towards the table where the history buff is sat.

I, of course, spin around to see what's caught her eye.

The fur coat woman is up off her chair, arms flying, head shaking so fast she'll make herself dizzy if she isn't careful.

"Who is that?" I hiss towards Connie.

"Lavinia." She whispers. "Lavinia Blackbottom."

"Blackbottom?" I ask with a childish smirk.

"Yes. Don't let her hear you, she can't stand people making fun of the family name."

I try to stifle my laughter and return my attention her way.

"You're insufferable, Lovey!" She exclaims, her voice loud enough for people - and spirits - at several tables to turn and look at her. I spot Patton a few tables over and give him a little wave.

"Lavinia, please. Sit down." Lovey, the historian, urges. He pulls on the sleeve of her fur and she yanks away from him, spilling coffee across the table.

"Oh look what you've done now! You wretched man! This is all nonsense."

Lovey looks around and clicks his fingers for a member of staff to clean up the mess. Ellie notices and ignores him. I knew I liked her.

"I'll discuss price. That was just an offer."

"It was an insult, not an offer!" Lavinia shouts. "An insult to the very name of Blackbottom!"

I have to look away to stop the giggles. How anyone could be so protective of such an awful name, I can only imagine. I think I'd have been a child bride to ditch the surname.

Ellie walks across towards their table.

"Ah, finally, the staff are here." Lovey says. "Y'all need to get this cleared up."

"I need you both to be quiet, you're disturbing the customers." Ellie says, eyes fierce, arms crossed.

"Well, I've never been so insulted!" Lavinia says. "I'm only in this... this... diner to lend you the credibility of having a Blackbottom's custom."

"We seem to be doing okay on our own, thank you." Ellie says, and she gestures around the crowded coffee house, where every customer is watching the scene unfold.

"And it's not a diner!" A voice calls out from a table towards the back.

"There's nothing wrong with a nice diner." Another voice calls.

Ellie rolls her eyes and walks back to the counter, leaving Lovey to rifle through his satchel bag to find a tissue and mop up the spilt coffee himself. Lavinia hovers by the table, awaiting an apology that nobody seems about to offer.

"I don't have to stay here!" She announces, waits a further few seconds for a reaction that doesn't come, and then storms out of the door.

It's a gorgeous, sunny day in Mystic Springs, and I expect she's regretting her wardrobe choice within two seconds of the heat greeting her out there.

"Well, what a character she is." I say, returning my attention to Connie.

"I can't believe you don't know her."

"Should I?"

"She's the great-granddaughter of the woman who first discovered Mystic Springs and set up home here. She - the great-grandmother - was the first Mayor here. Lavinia thinks she's something of a local celebrity."

"Well, that plan isn't working out too well for her." I quip.

Connie shrugs. "She's pretty irrelevant. It's hard to see what she does to add any value here, just waltzes around when she's not travelling and expects people to respect her more than they do."

"I think she adds a lot." A voice came from behind me. Atticus. I should have known he'd be around. He doesn't miss a trick. "It's good for the town to have a figurehead."

"I don't disagree with that." Connie says. "But I don't think Lavinia is the figurehead. Her great-grandmother sounds like an amazing woman, but our Lavinia's nothing more than a rich layabout."

"How did she get her money?" I ask. I'm always interested in how people get their money, mainly because I never had any when I was alive and I'm curious what I did wrong.

Connie shrugs. "Probably inherited."

"It doesn't hurt us to have a Blackbottom here. It's a little like the Royal Family, you Brits love having them!"

"I don't think you can compare Lavinia Blackbottom to the British Royal Family." Connie says.

"See what I mean!" Atticus says. "You're very defensive of them. God Save The Queen and all that. I love it!"

Atticus would love to be British, I think. He likes pomp and ceremony and there just isn't enough of it in small-town USA.

"You know." Atticus says, and he moves closer, his spirit face like an unfocused photograph. "I once had a dream that I married the Queen."

"Really?" I ask.

"Absolutely. It wasn't all I'd imagined. It turned out she was so used to servants and helpers, she wasn't really after a husband, just another assistant. I carried her bags for her, made her cups of tea, that kind of thing. It was a hoot living in Buckingham Palace, though. I'd like to have that dream again."

I glance at Connie, who looks as confused as I do by this confession.

"How, nice?" She says, always better at bemused small talk than me.

"Magnificent, it was. And oh the breakfasts! I can still taste the sausage now." Atticus says with a hearty laugh. A picture of him, sitting in a grand banquet hall in Buckingham Palace, spearing a sausage with an 18-carat gold fork pops into my head.

I guess there can't be any secrets in Mystic Springs now.

2

CONNIE

I've started to buy the newspaper.

I never used to, I didn't have the time. Or I'd buy it, but toss it into the trash three days later after accepting that I wouldn't be able to find the time to read it.

I tried an online subscription once, thinking I'd be more likely to read it in bite-size chunks on my phone, but even that didn't work. It turns out, I was one of those people who was so busy I didn't even have those five minute pockets of waiting-around time like lots of people do. I was just flat out busy, all day long.

But now, I have time.

And I'm at that stage in my life where the idea of an hour reading the newspaper with a cup of coffee sounds like heaven, even if the thing is full of bad news. The newspaper, not the coffee.

So my new routine is to walk across town to the news-stand, where the woman, Ling, greets me by name now.

Today, her grin is even bigger than normal.

"Connie! Good news day today!" She cries as I pootle across the road to her. I've taken Sage's advice and am wearing linen slacks and a t-shirt that shows my curves more than I'd like, but the woman nods approvingly at me. "Nice outfit. Suits you."

"Get out of town." I say, the sentence tumbling out of my mouth awkwardly, as if I'm impersonating someone else. I feel my cheeks flame. I've forgotten the etiquette for compliments. "What's the good news?"

"Here, see." Ling says in her broken English, and hands me a copy of the newspaper.

"This isn't good news." I say as I do a double take and reread the headline. "Town history unreliable according to journal discovery?"

"Says men set up Mystic Springs, not women." Ling says with a shrug. She's still grinning. "Lots of people interested in this! We sell lots of newspapers today."

"Ah, well, it's a good day for you and Bill then." I say. Ling's husband, who runs the newsstand with her, isn't around, as normal.

Ling moves closer to me and whispers, "You think it's true?"

"I don't know." I admit.

"I always hear Lavinia Blackbottom discover Mystic Springs."

"Me too." I say. "Her and a band of women she was leading across the country. Mystic Springs, home of girl power!"

My Spice Girls reference goes over her head but she's polite enough to smile anyway. I'm too British for America, sometimes.

"Men need to say everything thanks to them." Ling says, then flashes me a conspiratorial grin. Unlike her, I have no husband to remain loyal to, but I've met plenty of women in my time who like to claim credit they're not entitled to.

"Where is Bill, anyway?" I ask.

She lets out a hee-haw laugh. "Bill no fan of early mornings."

I glance at my watch. "It's ten thirty."

She shrugs. "Men."

I smile and hand over the change for my newspaper.

If this article is right, there will be uproar in Mystic Springs.

And I know the best place to go to hear the gossip.

Screamin' Beans is overflowing with locals, all buzzing with the drama of the newspaper story. I order a hot cocoa and manage to squeeze in to a spare seat on a table of four.

Lovey Lovegoode, the historian, sits across from me, nursing a tiny espresso cup in a large hand that shakes slightly. Next to him sits an out-of-towner, identifiable thanks to the keen business dress she wears and the reporter's notepad that's open in front of her. A journalist. Atticus will be beside himself with excitement.

Next to me, thankfully, is a chair holding all of the reporter's belongings. These tables are too tight for me to squeeze in this close to another person, but I don't mind pushing the bags over a little so I can fit comfortably.

I fold open my copy of the newspaper and read the article with interest. A historic journal has been discovered that records the founding of Mystic Springs and names a man, Wilson Bruiser, as the true pioneer who discovered the place. The article goes further, describing the women who up to now were accepted as founding the town, as Bruiser's followers, women blinded by his charms who were able to serve as staff for him but had no leadership skills.

"It's pretty wild, huh?" Lovey says, interrupting my reading. I glance up at him.

"Do you believe this?" I ask. Few people will offer a more informed opinion than the local historian. I got lucky finding this free seat, even if he is usually incredibly dull.

"I couldn't say without seeing the journal." He says. "As a historian, my work is in facts, not opinions. The newspaper version, almost certainly, will be embellished. But there could be a hint of the truth in it."

"I deal with facts too." The reporter says from behind the stiff collar of a bright red blouse. She holds out an arm towards me, and I shake her hand. "Jayne Simpleton."

"New Yorker?" I ask, detecting the accent.

"Born and raised." She says, a cheap ballpoint pen poised ready. "And you are?"

"Oh, I don't want to give a quote or anything." I say as I shift in my seat. Maybe I didn't get lucky sitting here.

"That's okay. We don't bite, ya know."

I smile. "It's Connie. Connie Winters."

"The psychic?"

"Medium... yes, that's me. Wait, how do you know my name?"

"It came up." She says. "I've been talking to as many people as I can, get a feel for the place. It helps. So, you see dead people?"

"I see spirits." I say with a cringe. "All of the local people do."

She smiles at me in a way that tells me she knows I'm crazy. "How fabulous for you. You didn't mention that you saw ghosts, Mr Lovegoode. Local historian sees the dead! I didn't get your first name?"

"Lovey." He says. "Lovey Lovegoode. So good, my parents named me twice."

She doesn't get the reference to New York, too busy jotting details down on her notepad.

"I'm serious." I say, my voice timid. "I don't want to be included in any newspaper articles."

"It could be great for your business." Jayne says with a sugary smile. "People love psychics."

"I don't need any more work, thanks." I say. It's taken me years to get to this reduced workload, and I don't plan on changing that.

"Hmm, suit yourself." She says. "So, Lovely Lovegoode, what can you tell me?"

"It's Lovey, not Lovely." He says, expression stern.

"And you're the historian? I understand you deal with facts, but you may be best placed to give an opinion first of all. What do you make of this article?"

"Honestly?" Lovey sneers, as if being asked for his opinion for a New York newspaper is beneath him. "I question whether the journal even exists. The newspaper doesn't name it's source, curiously. I wonder if, perhaps, a quiet news day caused someone to get a little creative with the truth."

"Interesting." Jayne says, with a glance at her notepad. Her handwriting is drunken hieroglyphics. "How about this man they name? Wilson Bruiser? Ever heard that name?"

"I can't possibly say." Lovey says. "I've come across far too many names for me to say whether I've come up against that particular fellow."

"But would it be fair to say that if he was a central role in the town's creation, you'd be familiar with his name?"

"No." Lovey says, adamantly. "Absolutely not. If he were a central role in the history books, I'd be familiar with his name. But the history books themselves are not always accurate. Those writing them naturally hold the power, and will often have their own agenda."

"So, you're saying, even if the journal exists, whatever it says may not be reliable?"

"Exactly." Lovey says. "That's always a factor to remember when dealing with any historical document."

"Interesting." Jayne says. It's her catchphrase, the word she goes to to buy her some time to finish writing, or consider her next question. I think back to a radio interview I did years ago. My first and last. I'd been terrified. The presenter, recognising my nerves, gave me a piece of advice I'd never forgotten.

Listen to the question, and answer with a long word, to buy yourself thinking time.

It's amazing how many people use that trick, I've realised. And not just on the radio or TV, but in day to day life.

"Don't you think?" Lovey asks, and I realise he is speaking to me.

"Absolutely." I say with a smile, not sure what I'm agreeing to.

"If I can only examine the journal, I can establish whether it's a genuine article, and then comment further." Lovey says. His eyes are fierce behind his designer specs. "I need the journal."

"We really need the person who found the journal to come forward." Jayne says.

"Nonsense." Lavinia Blackbottom's unmistakable voice comes from the doorway. I groan when I see her outfit.

"Excuse me?" Jayne asks.

"Lavinia Blackbottom, the fourth." Lavinia says, but she doesn't extend a hand to the reporter.

"What are you wearing?" The reporter asks, grabbing

her camera from one of the bags on the seat next to me. "Mind if I?"

She's snapping photographs before Lavinia can object, not that she would. She's wearing a waistcoat adorned with bundles of genuine $50 notes - her money coat.

"Are they real?"

"Of course!" Lavinia says. She plucks a note off of the bundle that covers her right breast. "Here, treat yourself."

"Erm." Jayne says, examining the note to see if it really is real. "Blackbottom, you say?"

"Great-granddaughter of Lavinia Blackbottom, founder and first Mayor of Mystic Springs. The news story is nonsense. Tosh! Everyone knows that great-grandmother set up this place."

"Come, come, sit down." Jayne says and scrabbles to move the bags from the seat. She eyes me and the way my ripples of flab hang over my own chair width, and pulls the spare chair away from me slightly.

Lavinia remains standing, after all that.

"I should have known you'd be all over the press." Lavinia says, eyeing Lovey.

"This fine lady required a seat."

"Has he told you the pressure he's been putting me under?"

"No." Jayne says, eyes wide, nose flaring at the sniff of a story. "Do go on."

"Well." Lavinia says, and as she runs a hand through her hair I spot what must be a Rolex on her skeletal wrist. "Lovey here seems to think that anything old should end up in his care, even if it doesn't belong to him."

"That's an outrageous lie!" Lovey roared, his booming voice attracting the attention of the people on the next table.

"Ms Simpleton, let me explain. I'll spare the dramatics and tell the truth."

"Are you suggesting I -"

"Here's what happened. I discovered that Miss Blackbottom has a rather rare collection of antique cash registers, and they quite piqued my attention."

"Cash registers?"

Lovey nods. "I worked in a general store as a boy, back home in the ghetto. It would be marvellous to own a collection like this one, more for sentimental value really. I offered a fair price and I was open to negotiation."

"The ghetto?" I ask. Lovey Lovegoode didn't look or sound like he came from any ghetto.

"Oh, not that again. This man wouldn't know a ghetto if he took a wrong turning and found himself in one. He went to Harvard, for goodness sake." Lavinia says with a brisk shake of her head.

Lovey's cheeks flush.

"Anyway, if you need any quotes or anything, it's me you'll be wanting to speak to. I'm happy to set the record straight." Lavinia says.

"Do you have any idea who has the journal?" Jayne asks.

"No." Lavinia says. "It might not even exist. People will do anything for five minutes of fame."

"They're not getting any fame, though." I say. "The article doesn't name them."

"They'll crawl out of the woodwork sooner or later with a story to sell." Lavinia says. The $50 notes on her jacket dance in the breeze as the front door opens.

"It's me." A timid voice calls.

I turn. The woman who stands before me is washed-out, her skin as grey as the clothes she wears. Three-day grease clings to her limp hair, but her face is extraordinarily pretty.

Descended from gypsies, if you listen to the rumours, which I of course don't.

"Emelza Shabley." Lavinia hisses.

"You two know each other?"

"She was staff." Lavinia spits. "Until I caught her with her fingers where they shouldn't have been."

I look at Emelza, whose grey skin manages not to flush with even a hint of colour.

"I bet she stole the journal from my personal belongings!" Lavinia exclaims.

"So you accept there is a journal, now?" Jayne Simpleton asks, and I notice that she's still snapping pictures as the scene unfolds. I bet she wishes she'd brought a cameraman with her to record this.

"Who knows." Lavinia says. "There may well be a journal, I just don't accept it says what this little runt is pretending it does."

"Emelza, I think the best thing is that you release the journal to me, as an independent third party." Lovey begins. Emelza's gaze flits between him and Lavinia before resting on me as the only impartial person at the table.

"What should I do?" She asks.

Jayne points the camera towards me then and I grab my handbag and hold it in front of my face. "Put the camera down, I've made it clear I don't want to be involved in this."

I peek over the top of the bag and see that the reporter's returned her camera to the table, so I cradle the bag in my lap. Ridiculous. I've never understood why some people are so desperate for media attention. Seeing my face in the newspaper sounds like something out of a nightmare.

Emelza is still gazing at me, the hopeless creature.

"How should I know what you should do?" I say, my tone more irritated than I intend. She flinches back from me, but

I'm not sure why she thinks I'm her comrade in this situation. I barely know the woman.

"Emelza, just let me review the journal, there's a good girl." Lovey says. I blink at how patronising he sounds. The reporter jots more random shapes down on her pad. I assume, in whatever mystical shorthand she uses, she's recording him saying good girl. "Look, how about I come over tonight, I believe I know your address. I'll pop over and take a look? And, of course, if you need money, I may be able to find a buyer for it."

Emelza looks like a woman who has always needed money and never had quite enough of it.

Jayne Simpleton picks up her camera again and flashes it too close in my direction.

"I'm going." I announce, not that anyone cares. They're all far too engrossed in the drama of the journal.

I rap on the door quietly, not wanting to wake the twins if it's nap time.

Adele opens the door a moment later, her face forming a weary smile when she sees me.

"Oh. Hi. Coffee?" She offers, leading me into the wide hallway. The house is silent.

"Only if you're making one?"

"I have baby twins. I'm always making one."

I laugh. "Are they asleep?"

"I've sent Taylor to his parents' with them for the night." She says as she flicks the kettle on.

"Everything okay?" I ask.

She cracks her knuckles and stifles a yawn.

I note how her hair is straighter than normal, and then see the subtle layer of make-up. Her clothes are smarter too.

So, this is what Adele looks like when she's not in mom mode.

"You look great, by the way." I say.

"Thanks." She says with a shrug. That's how to take a compliment! I need to remember that, on the off chance I ever get another. "I could barely remember how to contour, it's been so long."

"Ha, imagine." I say, and I suddenly feel uncomfortable in her presence. It was okay when she was the slightly dishevelled Adele, struggling being a newcomer in town with raising tiny twin babies. But this Adele is polished and well put-together. I'm taken over by insecurities that she may not want to be my friend anymore.

"Have you heard all this news about the journal?" Adele asks, handing me a cup of strong coffee. "Why do people care?"

"Oh, it's a big deal. The town's always been proud of its independent women roots."

Adele shrugs and gazes out of the lounge window. A teenage boy cycles past and throws a newspaper onto the lawn next door. "Sounds like a quiet news day."

"Well, this ain't New York any more." I say lightly.

"Tell me about it." She mutters.

"Hey." I say, sensing that something is wrong. "Why don't we grab some dinner together tonight?"

She turns to me and bites her lip, then nods. "I was going to just catch up on some sleep, but sure. Let's do that."

"You can still be in bed early?" I ask, wondering if I'm pushing too hard, forcing myself on her.

"Okay." She agrees, and I try to ignore the feeling that she's agreeing out of courtesy rather than desire to spend a grown-up meal together.

3

SAGE

I could have heard the scream from across the other side of town, okay? The fact that I wasn't across town doesn't matter. Yes, I was in a bush, very close to where the scream came from, but that's really not the point. Don't get hung up on it.

You could say, it's lucky I was so close.

And yes, I was with Patton. In a bush. In the dark.

Like I say, concentrate on the important bits, please.

He's up and off like a greyhound, and I go after him. This place is pretty deserted. It's basically a field out on the edge of town. There aren't even street lights out here, which makes it pretty hard to know where I'm racing off to. Luckily, spirits emit a slight glow, so I can make out Patton ahead and try to keep up with him as best I can.

Across the field from us, there's a gypsy waggon, a William Wheeler Showman's waggon in crimson lake and cream, complete with gold leaf curlicues. The door is open, and it's like stepping back in time. Incredibly neat, and more spacious than it appears from the outside, the narrow interior split into a living area, with kitchen appliances on the left-hand side and the right taken up with storage units, topped with cushions to create a seating bench. Past the living area, there's a small bed, and atop the bed, there's a small grey-faced woman, eyes open, a bloodied dagger protruding from her back.

"Bloody typical." Patton moans. "He only rocked up five minutes ago and he's already on holiday."

"He's allowed a day off." I say, but Patton glares at me for making that comment, so I shut up.

We've exited the crime scene, as the Showman's waggon now is, and called the Sheriff, Taylor Morton, but apparently he's out of town for the night.

"You don't need him anyway." I say with a flutter of my eyelashes. Patton's wearing his Sheriff's uniform, the old-fashioned version that was still being worn before he died. My stomach's doing flips and I'm not sure if it's down to how cute he looks or the memory of the woman in the waggon.

"We need to search the area." Patton says. "But it's too dark. We need resources out here."

A screech of sirens in the distance ring out.

"Oh great, the ambulance." Patton says, his voice dripping with sarcasm.

"You think she's already...?"

"Dead? I'd be amazed if not. Poor woman."

"Do you know her?"

"Not her, but the only people living out here for decades have been the Shabley family, she could be one of them."

"Gypsies? I didn't even know gypsies existed."

Patton frowns at me. "Of course they do."

"So she's just moving around from place to place?" I ask.

"No." He explains. "This site has been used by them for

decades, like I say. Occasionally someone starts a petition wanting them to be moved on, but they don't normally succeed. Most people don't mind them being out here."

"Them?"

"There's usually more waggons than this. It's strange that the others would go and whoever this is would stay."

"Maybe she stayed to make sure the land was kept for the others?"

"Could be." Patton agrees. "Come on, let's do a search of the area now the ambulance crew are here."

The ambulance, sent from out of town, pulls up next to the waggon and the paramedics climb out, look around the area and disappear into the waggon.

"Let's stay together?" I ask, feeling spooked.

"Of course." He says, and he slips his hand into mine.

The waggon sits on a patch of land that's been given up to nature for decades. The grass is overgrown and the risk of us coming across a snake is, in my head, at least 100%.

In the dark of night, we can see the lights from the town in the distance, but nothing of the grass itself.

"This is useless." Patton says, with a sigh. "Whoever did this will have got away by now. Let's spread the word and come back in the morning. We can bring a team, if Taylor isn't back."

"Sounds good." I say. Anything that involves me leaving the dark field and returning to the town sounds good right now.

I don't know if Connie will be home yet from her dinner with Adele Morton, and I don't feel like risking an empty house, so I suggest to Patton that we go over to the Baker house, where the spirits tend to hang out.

"Sure." He says with a shrug, but his mind is focused on the case. The excitement he felt earlier in the evening to be with me has gone. The man is never off duty.

The lights are on at the Baker house and we're greeted with a cheer as we walk in together. Spirits can be so immature. Like they've never seen a man and a woman be friends before, huh?

"What's wrong?" Atticus, the dead Mayor, asks Patton right away, pausing his game of chess.

"Someone's been killed tonight." Patton whispers.

Atticus groans. "Someone?"

"Not Mariam." I say, to his relief. He worries about his daughter like you wouldn't believe. "It's some gyspy."

"Emelza?" He asks. "She's the only one left. Or, she was."

"Maybe." I say.

"What do you know about her?" Patton asks Atticus. The three of us move out of the living room, away from the watchful gaze of other spirits, and out onto the front lawn. The streets are empty. The town has retired to bed, unaware of what's happened in a waggon across town.

"Not much." He says. "She kept herself to herself. She was always writing complaint letters. I must have had three dozen from her when I was Mayor."

"Complaining about what?"

"Anything!" He exclaims. "The town being too noisy, town people interfering on her land - even though it wasn't her land. The woman would complain about anything she could think of."

"So, she wasn't popular I'm guessing?"

"Definitely not. Most people couldn't stand her. Rumour had it she was a thief."

"No end of suspects, then, to want her dead." Patton says.

"Where's Morton?"

"Taylor's on holiday." Patton says with a sneer.

"He's away for one night. He'll be back tomorrow and we can hand this over to him and carry on relaxing." I say, hoping my voice is seductive in a subtle enough tone that only Patton will notice.

"Well, erm..." Atticus stumbles over his words and blushes. "You young uns probably don't want me hanging around."

Oops.

"I'm glad you're here." Patton says and my face drops. "We need to work on this together. Taylor's too new in town to solve a murder. He doesn't understand the way things work here."

Atticus nods thoughtfully. "The three of us, then. We'll crack the case."

I try to force a smile.

I drift off to sleep back in the living room, leaving Atticus and Patton to talk about the case and devise a strategy. I'm sulking, I know that, and I know that my foiled plans for date night don't make me the victim in this situation... but I still kind of feel like the victim.

I'm thrown out of my dreams by a chill that runs across me, and I jump up to a sitting position on the couch. The front door of the Baker house has burst wide open, and a gale is blowing its way inside, even though the living room door is closed.

"What's that?" I ask.

Patton silences me with a look and goes to the living room door, and pulls it open with a determined yank.

A tall, regal spirit stands before Patton, his hair white,

forehead dabbled with liver spots, fatty bags under his dark eyes. He wears a blazer, shirt and bow tie, and is missing his left hand.

"May I enter, fine chap?" He asks, fixing a broad smile towards Patton.

"You are?"

"Wilson Bruiser, the one and only! Heard my name being mentioned around town, thought I'd come and say hallo." He says. He notices me and makes a beeline for me, planting himself next to me on the couch and holding out his one hand. "Well, hallo indeed."

"Why are you faking a British accent?" I ask.

He descends into a laughter that is as much spluttering coughs as actual laughs. "I say, you're a sharp lassie!"

"Now Scottish?" I ask. "Where are you from?"

"A bit of everywhere, so I am."

"Irish? This is getting tiresome." I complain, although there's something quite captivating about him for an older man.

"Forgive me, it's been too long since I socialised with a beautiful woman."

"What are you here for?" Patton barks across at him as he returns to a couch. I sit back and smile. Two men fighting over me was always one of my favourite things to watch; better than any TV show.

"Haven't you heard? The locals have become obsessed with me. I thought they'd like to meet the man, the myth, the legend."

"Modest, then?" Patton asks.

"I see no need for modesty. Perhaps you wouldn't if you were as fine a specimen as I am. Now, let me take the name of my new lady friend."

"I'm Sage. Sage Shaw." I say. "And this is Patton Davey, he was the Sheriff."

"A rule follower, then? Makes sense. I'm more of a maverick."

"Is that right." Patton mumbles.

Atticus appears then and I yawn as the men make the introductions again.

"A woman found my journal." Wilson says. "I was the founder of Mystic Springs, I documented it all."

"No, you weren't. The founder of Mystic Springs was a woman, in an all-woman group. Lavinia Blackbottom."

"Lavinia, yes, I remember the old cow." He says. "She was obsessed with me! They all were, of course, but she was the worst. Insufferable. Wouldn't give me a minute's peace."

"You knew Lavinia?" Atticus asks. He's deep in thought, pacing the room.

"Of course I did, she was one of my helpers."

"That's not the story we all know." Patton says.

"Doesn't surprise me, she was a terrible attention seeker. But I wrote it all down, in a journal. I buried it out of town so those witches couldn't steal it."

"Hold on." I say. "Do you know the name of the woman who found it?"

"Shabley, I think. That's what I've heard."

"Oh, God." I groan.

"What, dear girl? You're too beautiful to be sad. Here, sit closer."

"Emelza Shabley was killed tonight."

"Oh!" Wilson says. "How exciting! Nothing like that happened in my day, worse luck."

"It's not exciting." Patton says, with a look towards Wilson's missing hand. "And it looks like it wasn't all peace and quiet in your day."

"Oh, don't be such a rotter! And yes, yes, good point! You should have seen the state of the other men!"

"Men, plural?"

"A whole army of them! I showed them. Now, Sage, what do you say? Fancy showing me to a bedroom?"

I feel myself blush at his proposition, which is strange because I'm no stranger to them. "There's no way you're getting me anywhere near a bedroom."

"Your loss." He says with a grin and a shrug of his broad shoulders.

In the morning, there's no sign of Wilson Bruiser and I'm surprised to realise that I feel disappointed. There was something exciting about him.

Patton notices me looking distracted and I flash him a reassuring smile.

"I'll head across to the Morton house soon, want to come?"

"Erm..." I say. "I should update Connie, really."

"Fine." He says.

"What's wrong?"

"You fell asleep with that awful man draped all over you." Patton says with a shake of his head. "I think you should keep away from him, Sage."

"Jealous?"

"No! Why would I be? We're only friends. You're married, remember." He says. Ouch, that hurts. Yes, I'm married, but only because there's no way for ghosts to divorce. Choose a bad 'un while you're alive and you're stuck with them for an eternal afterlife? I don't think so! My husband isn't a bad 'un, though, just a fairly boring one. One lifetime was enough with him, thank you very much.

"Sorry. That was uncalled for. Maybe I am a bit jealous." Patton says.

"Well, you've got no reason to be." I say, although as he talks I'm comparing the steady lilt of his own American accent with the rollercoaster of dialects of Wilson.

"Come on then, shall we walk together?"

"I'm not ready yet." I say, which is a blatant lie. "I'll see you later."

Patton nods and gets up, leaves the house. I can see him float down the street, shoulders down, head bowed. I shouldn't like it at all, this power I have over men, but it's like there's a flirtatious demon inside me who just can't resist the thrill of a man's attention.

I sit back and close my eyes, picturing Wilson and Patton.

There's no competition, really.

Patton's a fine man, committed to his work. Honest, upstanding, and apparently interested in me and nobody else.

No choice at all.

I jump up and chase Patton as quick as I can.

"Change your mind?" He asks with a tight smile.

"I figure I can tell Connie after we see Taylor."

He nods.

"Thank you." I say.

"What for?"

"Looking out for me."

"That's my job." He says. Silence. Then, "I'm sorry for what I said, about you being married."

"Well, I am."

"I know, but I... I shouldn't have raised it like that."

"Does it bother you?" I ask.

"Of course not." He says. "Although I wonder if it would

bother your husband, you know, knowing that we're friends like this."

"He's moved on, just like I have." I say.

Patton gives me a real smile then, and his chiseled jaw makes my stomach flip.

Connie has always said I'm boy mad. Boy mad, then man mad.

As if it's a bad thing.

When there are men like Patton Davey around, why on Earth wouldn't I be man mad?

Taylor answers the door, and he looks more dead than I do.

"What?"

"You haven't heard?" Patton asks. "Don't you keep up to date when you're off shift?"

"I was in the hospital all night."

"I thought you were out of town?"

"Should have been. One of the babies got ill, had to go to the emergency room. What's happened?"

"Oh, wow." Patton says, and I guess he's feeling like the worst person in the world right now. "I'm sorry, everything okay?"

"It's going to be."

"Someone was killed last night."

"Argh." Taylor says and runs his hands through his hair. "You're kidding me. The one night I..."

"It's okay." I soothe. "Don't worry. We happened to be out there, we found the person, but whoever did it got away."

"Who's the victim?"

"We think it's Emelza Shabley."

"The woman who found that journal?"

Patton nods. "There's only one waggon left across town

and she was in it. I don't know the woman but I think it must be her."

"Cause of death?"

"Stabbed by some kind of dagger. EMTs came pretty quick from out of town."

"Who do they think called it in?"

"I don't know, that's a good question." Patton says. "I probably gave my name automatically, but I don't remember for sure."

"Well, that doesn't matter. You got there afterwards?"

"We heard the scream." I say. "Whoever did it must have disturbed her, she screamed, and then by the time we got across there, it was too late."

"Hmm." Taylor says. "Where were you exactly? There's nothing out there."

"We were -"

"Walking. Walking in the field." I say with a splutter.

Taylor raises an eyebrow but doesn't press the point. "You got there how quick after the scream?"

"Seconds. Maybe five." Patton says.

"Something doesn't add up." Taylor says. "There's nothing out there, it's deserted. You say that's the only waggon? So nobody around. But the person had gone within five seconds? Why would they go so fast?"

"She screamed." I repeat. "The person will be worried someone heard that scream."

"But five seconds, to stab someone, make sure they're dead, and get away?"

"Maybe my time isn't exact, maybe it was more than five seconds."

"Hmm."

"What are you thinking, Sheriff?" Patton asks.

"I'm not thinking anything clear yet. I need to go and

bring my baby home from hospital, get him settled with Adele, and then I can try and wrap my head around this."

"Of course."

"If we can help..."

"I'll let you know." Taylor says. "Thanks, for letting me know."

We take the cue and leave the house, looking glumly at each other until Taylor comes back to the front door.

"Patton?" He calls.

Patton turns to face him.

"Good work, Sheriff." Taylor says, and Patton's chest inflates.

Back at home, Connie sits at the kitchen table, nursing a mug of cocoa.

She glares at me as soon as I close the door.

"Where the hell have you been?" She shouts. "If you're going to be staying under my roof, you need to tell me if you're not coming home. I've been worried sick."

"Woah!" I exclaim. "Sorry, mom! First of all, I thought you were out last night? Second, your friend Adele's baby is in hospital. And third, I discovered a dead body last night."

"A body? Who?"

"Emelza Shabley. Someone stabbed her with some old dagger last night in her waggon."

"Last night? Lovey Lovegoode was going to see her last night. I heard it being arranged."

4

CONNIE

*I*t comes as no surprise that Sage wants me to help her investigate.

Less than five minutes after she's wandered back in the house stinking of aftershave, she's pleading with me to help her. And I'm in no mood to.

She needs to learn to follow the rules and have some respect for someone other than herself. She treats this place like her home, and she treats me like her skivvy. It needs to change.

I've been up since 7am enjoying the quiet, and my thoughts kept coming back to how she takes advantage of my good nature. And how it has to stop.

"Don't glare at me like that." She says. I didn't know I was glaring, but she's probably right.

"I'm not getting involved, Sage. And you shouldn't either."

"I kind of already am involved." She says, like a petulant teenager.

"And I don't even want to know how you got involved, being out in a field with a man after dark."

"Oh, lighten up. You should go out in a field with a man after dark yourself, it might make you a bit less serious. In fact, there's an eligible bachelor just arrived in town. He's dead, but I wouldn't kick him out of bed. Wilson Bruiser. What a name."

"Wilson Bruiser?" I ask. "He's the man named in the journal that Emelza found. When did he turn up?"

"Late last night, he was at the Baker house making moves on me."

"Oh Sage, not everything has to be about you." I say through gritted teeth. "There won't be any need for either of us to get involved, this case sounds black and white."

"It does?"

"Wilson Bruiser obviously came back for his journal. Emelza refused to give it to him and he killed her. Case closed."

"Why would he want it back? It's getting attention for him now anyway. He seems awfully vain."

"I'm not getting drawn into it." I say. "That's my guess of what happened, we'll see what Taylor thinks of it all."

Sage nods.

"And you shouldn't joke about ill babies, that's a terrible thing to do."

"Huh? I wasn't joking. One of the twins has just been discharged, Taylor was going across to bring them all home."

"What?" I say, and I'm on my feet immediately. "What was wrong?"

"No idea. But it's going to be okay, apparently."

"Ugh, Sage, why didn't you say? I need to go and see Adele."

. . .

I reach their house just as Adele steps out of the car.

She's wrought with worry, her face pale and her hair limp around her face. I immediately regret my wish that she'd return to the more plain version of herself.

"What can I do?"

"There's been a murder." Taylor says, appearing from the other side of the car with a baby in a car seat. "I have to go to work. Can you stay? Please?"

"Of course." I say, glad again that my diary is quieter now. I reach out for the car seat. "Here, let me take that. You go. Sage told me about Emelza."

"It's a terrible business." He says, passing the car seat across to me. I notice that it's Scarlett I'm carrying. Adele has reached into the car and grabbed Axel from his car seat. She holds him tight to her chest. His colour is off and his breathing is ragged.

"You go, we'll be fine." I say with more confidence than I possess. I love babies, but I'm not sure I have enough experience with them for this.

"I wasn't there." Adele says as we enter the house. I lock it behind us.

"He's going to be okay?"

"He's going to be fine. Just needs some rest. But I wasn't there. I came home and turned off my phone, I was asleep within ten seconds."

"It's okay." I soothe. Our dinner out had been a disaster. Adele had been distracted all evening, before quickly paying the tab after our mains. Not even a glance at a dessert menu. She'd apologised, of course, and I'd reminded her that all she'd wanted to do was sleep the free time away. I should have let her. The woman's clearly exhausted.

. . .

After a lunch of pre-packed pesto spaghetti salads for us and milk for the twins, a miracle happens and both babies fall asleep. I force Adele to go and get a shower and a nap herself, and I settle myself on the couch with the remote control while the babies snooze in their bassinets.

The first channel that comes on is a regional news station, and I'm not surprised at all to see that Adele is doing her best to keep up to date with world events even while being such a new mom.

I gasp as a familiar face appears on screen.

"And now we're joined by Lavinia Blackbottom the fourth, who resides in Mystic Springs. Ms Blackbottom is a passionate advocate for women's rights and independence and is here as part of our Women's Week. Ms Blackbottom, welcome."

Lavinia sits on a high stool in a short skirt, her tanned legs crossed and feet slipped into dangerously high heels. Thankfully, she's not wearing the money coat.

"Yes, yes, fabulous to be here to share my important message with your viewers."

"Ms Blackbottom, you're the great-granddaughter of Lavinia Blackbottom, founder and first Mayor of Mystic Springs. We understand that she was part of an all-female group who discovered and founded the town. So, it seems, female independence is in your blood?"

"Of course. My great-grandmother was a true leader, an independent woman in every sense, and I have followed in her footsteps while also paving my own way and carrying the torch of the Blackbottom name."

"Quite." The presenter says.

"What a load of rubbish." I say quietly, not wanting to disturb the babies. The sound of the shower upstairs has stopped, and I hope that Adele has curled up in bed and is drifting off to sleep.

"What does it mean to you, to be an independent woman?"

"Well, it's all about not relying on anyone else." Lavinia says.

"Emotionally, financially..." The presenter says.

"Every way, yes yes."

"Is that easier to do when you have an inherited wealth?"

"Well, I wouldn't know. I have no inherited wealth."

"Oh, sorry, I assumed..."

"People always assume and it's a dangerous game. My family have over the generations been rewarded dreadfully in financial terms for their devotion to Mystic Springs."

"Well, it's been fascinating speaking to you today, Lavinia. How important would you say it is for women to support and encourage each other in life?"

"It's vital." Lavinia says, addressing the camera. "I've never understood the need some women feel to tear other women down. We are the greater sex, that much is obvious, and yet we hold ourselves back by engaging in petty squabbles. Every woman should make it her mission to speak only of life and power and strength about her fellow women. That is how we claim our true collective power and, really, there's no stopping us then. And I think we all know that women ruling the world would see a very different type of world, indeed."

"Well, if we can steer away from politics..." The presenter says, antsy.

"We are living in dark times." Lavinia ploughs ahead. "Women leadership at the highest levels, the highest levels of business and politics, is the answer. Men have held the control for too long and look at the God-awful mess they've got us into!"

"Well, thank you, some very interesting comments here. Ms Blackbottom, news is just reaching us of a murder in your home town, could you comment on that for us?"

Lavinia's face transforms, a fleck of something unreadable, for a moment, and then it passes.

"A woman has been killed in Mystic Springs. This is breaking news." The reporter says, a hand to their ear to hear the news being fed to him. "We can confirm that a Ms Emelza Shabley has been stabbed to death. This is clearly awful, awful news, coming straight from a town devoted to women's rights."

"Devoted to women's rights?" I scoff. "She's devoted to her own PR."

But I want to see her reaction, which I'm told will come right after the adverts, which try to convince me that I should join a new gym, set up my own website, and change my insurance provider. And then, the news returns. Lavinia stares straight in to the camera, her gaze too intense.

"I'm joined, in a happy coincidence, by Ms Lavinia Blackbottom the fourth, descendant of the founder and first Mayor of Mystic Springs. Ms Blackbottom, we're hearing breaking news that a woman from your town, an Emelza Shabley, has been stabbed to death. Can we get a comment to that?"

Lavinia looks at the presenter, and then back at the camera, and then disappears to the right as her body topples from the high stool. A bang can be heard off screen and then the presenter jumps up, reaction delayed, and shouts, *we need a medic out here!*

. . .

It's hard to say what's the bigger news in town.

Emelza's murder or Lavinia's collapse on live TV. As concerned as people are about a murder happening in town, most of the residents agree that this is the first time in living memory that Lavinia Blackbottom has appeared to be anything other than perfectly presented, and so the collapse itself takes up much of the conversation.

I've returned to Screamin' Beans after Adele insisted that she would be fine with both babies.

"Soooooooo…" Sage coos as she perches on the seat next to me. Luckily, the coffee house is quiet enough that I've got a table for two to myself. Or I did have, before Sage arrived.

"So what?" I bark. I'm still grumpy with her for her disappearing act.

"Will you help investigate?"

"Ugh, you're still banging on about that? Don't you ever take the hint?"

"Wow, you're in a foul mood."

I am, I realise. I'm in a much more foul mood than Sage staying out overnight warrants. What's wrong with me?

"You know what I think?" Sage says, not pausing to see if I want to hear her thoughts. "I think all this extra time is bad for you."

I sigh. "I think you might be right."

"You do?"

I nod. "I don't know what's wrong with me. Maybe I'm just not used to this free time."

"Help me investigate, then. That'll give you something to do."

"I'll think about it." I agree. "I've got a client appointment tomorrow, that might be all I need to get my mojo back."

The client is an out of towner, as most of them are now.

It will be the first appointment I've had in a week, and I'm looking forward to connecting the person with their loved one. Well, hopefully. There's never a guarantee that the spirit will show up just because I ask them to.

"Is anything else going on?" Sage asks.

"Erm? Nooooooo." I say slowly, struck by how unusual the question is.

"Oh, good. Well, let me tell you about Wilson Bruiser."

I roll my eyes. Typical Sage, feigning interest in me before getting the conversation back to herself.

"Actually, maybe I would like to talk about me some more." I snap.

"You know what, I'm going to go. You're no fun to be around today." She says, and that's it, she's gone.

I check on Adele and the twins in the evening and gasp when Taylor opens the front door.

"I thought you'd be at work." I say.

"I did what I had to, I wanted to be home with Axel."

"How's it going? Any news?"

"Not yet." He says. "Early days. Want to come in?"

"I just thought I'd see if Adele needed any help, but if she's got you I'm sure everything's in hand."

He gives a small laugh. "I'm sure she'd say different, but yeah, I think things are okay. Thanks again for today."

"Anytime. Give those babies a kiss from me, yeah?"

He nods. "Connie, you're not thinking of investigating, are you?"

"No." I say. "I'm enjoying some rare peace and quiet."

"Hmm." He says, unconvinced.

5

SAGE

"We need some leads." Patton says, pacing around the living room of the Baker house. "Morton's too distracted with his poorly baby, which I'm not criticising him for, but everyone knows that time is of the essence in a murder case. Evidence is quite literally disappearing minute by minute."

"Connie said that Lovey Lovegoode was visiting Emelza the night she died."

"Lovey Lovegoode? What kind of name is that? That has to be fake." Atticus says, joining them.

"Says Atticus Hornblower." Patton says with an eye roll. "I've got the most normal name here."

"Sage Shaw is normal!" I object.

"No it isn't." Patton says. "A woman like you shouldn't have a plain name, anyway."

I feel myself smile. He's still been a little distant with me, since Wilson Bruiser turned up, but I can feel the ice thawing. It's impossible to stay mad at me for long, I'm adorable.

"Lovey's the local historian. He was desperate to get his hands on the journal, Connie says."

"Well, that's motive. And opportunity." Atticus says.

"And, even more. The dagger was old. Like, antique old. I bet this guy collects antiques?"

"I couldn't say." I admit. "He might, but we'd have to ask around. Or check his house."

Atticus and Patton both look at me with urgency.

"With permission, of course." I say. Spirits can't enter private dwellings without the resident's permission. That's the biggest rule for spirits in Mystic Springs. It's why we all hang out here, in the abandoned Baker house. The rule gets broken occasionally, of course. If you ask me, a murder investigation should allow the rules to be relaxed a little, but it appears nobody is asking me.

"He won't give permission." Patton says. "Morton needs to get a search warrant."

"And as slow as he's moving, any evidence will be long gone."

"The dagger was still in her back. Surely it just needs testing for DNA?" I say, thinking back to the gruesome sight of Emelza Shabley, eyes open, on her bed.

"You'd be surprised how often a killer manages not to leave DNA." Patton says.

"I would." I say. "I couldn't leave a room when I was alive without leaving stray hairs everywhere."

"The trouble is, if there's no DNA, suspicion will fall on us spirits." Atticus says.

"It could be a spirit."

"Connie thinks it's Wilson Bruiser."

"Makes sense." Patton says, too quickly.

"I don't think we should give up on Lovey Lovegoode." Atticus says. "He's giving a talk tonight in the town hall, maybe some of us should go."

"Great idea." Patton says.

"I have plans." Atticus says. "With Mariam."

"Me and you then, Sage?" Patton asks, and his smile reveals the dimple in his cheek that I adore. I'd say yes to any invitation from this man, I think.

The town hall is full of people who look as if they're ready to die.

I mean, not just one foot in the grave. I'm talking about people who have only got their noses left above the soil.

Barely alive, they are.

Maybe that's why Lovey's keeping his presentation so boring, because any sudden surprises might just kill off his audience.

Patton and I are the youngest in the audience by at least 80 years I reckon.

We sit at the back, where a few other spirits have gathered, and I prepare to be bored to sleep.

If Lovey cares about his topic at all, he's hiding it well.

He even breaks off for a yawn in parts.

I drift off to sleep until Patton elbows me in the ribs.

"Ouch!" I hiss at him, too loud. At least three people in the audience hear and clutch their chests. I'm joking, I'm joking. Barely.

"Sorry. He's wrapping up now, it's question time."

"I don't think I have any, other than how anyone stayed awake through that!"

Patton grins. "You're a heavy snorer, you know."

"Get lost, I've never snored in my life."

"Well, maybe you started in the afterlife."

I roll my eyes, enjoying the banter.

"Mr Lovegoode? I was interested in your thoughts on the claims that Lavinia Blackbottom didn't found Mystic

Springs, after all?" An elderly voice warbles from the front row.

"An excellent question." Lovey says. His deep brown skin perspires as he talks. "One that I don't feel able to comment on."

"Weren't you checking the journal?" The warbler persists.

"No, no." He says, flustered. "Any other questions? It's been a long evening, and no AC in here, let's call it a night."

"That's odd." Patton whispers.

Lovey gathers together his papers as a ripple of dissatisfaction passes through the crowd. The almost dead begin to stand and slowly, oh so slowly, walk up the centre aisle and towards the door at the back. One of them, a tiny woman with an almost bald head, spots me and Patton and shakes her head.

"They're everywhere!" She moans, clearly unhappy with her new gift of being able to see the dead.

"Boo!" I call out, and to my amusement, the woman actually jumps. Like, her whole body lifts off of the floor. Must be the most exercise the old bat has had in years.

"Sage, careful." Patton whispers, and he's so close to my ear that my belly starts to flip again.

"Are you flirting with me on purpose, Sheriff?" I ask, because the direct approach always shocks the good guys. He blinks at me and doesn't reply. "Oh, I'm teasing you. Come on, let's get out of here."

"No, let's stay." He says, and for a minute I think he's wanting to recreate his teenage dreams of smooching on the back row. "Something isn't right here. He was desperate for that journal, and now he's trying to distance himself from the whole thing. Why would he do that?"

"Well, he'd do it if he was the killer." I say.

"Exactly." Patton says.

"Shall we ask him?"

"No!" He exclaims. "Let's just keep an eye on him."

Lovey Lovegoode wipes his gleaming forehead with a handkerchief that he pulls from his trouser pocket, then gathers up his belongings and makes a quick exit. I look to Patton for help.

"Let's go." Patton whispers, and we set out to follow the historian.

As soon as he passes Bill's, the expensive supermarket, and doesn't go in, we know where he's heading. There's nowhere else to go, once you've passed Bill's, unless you're heading out of town which would make no sense on foot.

We trail him, staying quiet and keeping a distance. The evening is sticky with humidity and the roads are empty, people probably hiding indoors where they can run their fans and keep cool.

"This was so much easier when people couldn't see us." I whisper.

"Yeah, it was an unfair advantage, though." Patton says. "You can see why things had to change."

Lovey crosses the street and creeps across the field, approaching the waggon cautiously, but astonishingly he doesn't look behind him to check he hasn't been followed. We keep our distance and watch as he takes out the hand-kerchief to cover the doorknob and then opens the door.

"What is he doing? Trying to frame himself? His sweat's all over that thing." Patton whispers.

"No, that one was tartan. This one's checked."

"There's a difference?" He asks.

"You're such a man." I groan. "How come this place isn't taped off?"

"I guess Morton dropped the ball." Patton says with a grim shake of his head.

"Well, he does have a sick baby."

"It's no excuse. He should have asked someone else to do it if his head's not in the game."

The door closes behind Lovey and we glance at each other, unsure what to do. Now that we can be seen, it's not as easy to go up to a window and spy.

"We're going to have to have a look." Patton says, reading my mind. "I'll do it."

I follow him across to the side of the waggon and realise, in daylight, just how intricate it is. "This thing is beautiful. It must have cost loads."

"It'll have been in the family generations. Probably a wedding present originally."

"Nice." I say as Patton approaches the window. I crouch down so I'm not visible. I'm not going to tell Patton this, but when I got married the nicest gift I had was a throw blanket from a department store. From Connie, actually. There weren't many other presents, or wedding guests. I'd surrounded myself by then with adoring men, and none of them were ready to celebrate me choosing someone who wasn't them.

Patton peeks inside the waggon with half an eyeball, moves back, then looks again.

"It's okay, his back's to me. He's wiping prints away." Patton explains.

"He's what?"

"Getting rid of fingerprints. It's what criminals do, he must not have had time last night."

"Because he panicked and ran."

"Exactly."

"Where's he wiping?"

"Drawer handles, it looks like he really cased the joint."

"Looking for the journal."

Patton darts away from the window and grabs my hand, pulls me away from the waggon. "Quick, he's coming out. Hide."

We dart down into the long grass just as the waggon door opens and Lovey re-appears. He glances from side to side, then covers his hand with the handkerchief and closes the door. He walks quickly through the grass, but not so fast as to cause suspicion if anyone sees him. He's out of sight then, and I rise to my feet.

"So, we found our killer?" I say with a grin, heady with adrenaline.

"I guess so." Patton agrees.

"We don't need your help, after all." I say, just as Connie takes a sip of her coffee. I've returned home, walked right to the veranda by Patton, who bid me goodnight with a chastely kiss on the cheek, his musky scent lingering long after he'd gone.

She looks at me sharply but manages not to spit her drink out.

"Excuse me?"

"Your help, with the murder. We've solved the case."

"Who is we?"

"Me and Patton." I say with a shrug.

"You and Patton have solved the murder? Nothing to do with Sheriff Morton?"

"Well, between me and you.." I say, "he's been more

harm than good. His mind is totally with that sick baby. He didn't even tape off the waggon as a crime scene."

Connie groans. "Tell me you haven't been out there."

"Someone had to investigate, Connie. You made it clear you didn't want to."

She takes a deep breath, composes herself. She's wearing a t-shirt that shows off one, two, three rolls of stomach flab. A triple muffin top. And yet she still looks better than she did in the tents.

"You look nice, by the way." I say.

She eyes me, then relaxes her shoulders, lets out a breath and meets my gaze. "Thank you."

I laugh. "What was that about?"

"I'm practicing accepting compliments."

"Ahh... been getting a few, have you? I told you this was a better look."

Her cheeks flush. "Well, a couple maybe. I can't say I feel comfortable with my body on display like this."

"Connie, you look fine. You just need more confidence. And maybe a bit of an upper lip wax."

She rolls her eyes. "I knew you being nice to me couldn't last long."

I hold up my hands in protest. "I'm trying to help you!"

"Anyway." She says, and now I've mentioned it, I can't stop looking at the light brown caterpillar under her nose. Maybe I can wax her in her sleep. "Who did it?"

"Oh, yeah, that. It was Lovey."

"The historian?" Connie asks. She stands and flicks on the kettle, makes another coffee. "He did it to get the journal?"

I nod.

"What's the plan now? What does Sheriff Morton think?"

"We haven't told him yet. We only worked it out tonight. Wanna come over and see his reaction with us in the morning?"

"Maybe." She says. "I've got a client, though."

I shrug. "Your choice."

When I go out to fetch the milk the next morning, as if I'm staff, Patton's on the verandah, sitting in Connie's rocker.

"Hey, you been out here all night?" I joke.

He nods, bleary-eyed.

"You're serious?"

"I was pretty sure we weren't seen last night but I wanted to make totally sure you were okay. I started walking away but it didn't feel right. I needed to protect you, and Connie."

"Wow." I say, and my stomach flips. What a guy.

"Shall we go across to see Morton?"

"Let me just finish my errands." I say with a dramatic flourish and an eye roll. "Come in."

"Morning, Connie." Patton says as he floats inside.

Connie's in the kitchen, head in the fridge, and I hear a bang from within. "Ow!"

"Are you okay?"

She appears from the fridge and holds her head. "You made me jump, Patton."

"Sorry, ma'am." He says.

"You're grouchy." I say.

"I know." She says, and I shrug and leave the milk on the counter. Ain't no point talking to her when she's in a mood.

"Are you going to see Sheriff Morton?"

"Yep." I say, already floating back across towards the front door.

"I thought I was coming with you." Connie asks, her voice small and wounded.

"You said you've got your client so you can't. Come on, if you're coming." I snap, which is unlike me. I'm usually the height of chill, as the cool kids would say.

"It's fine, you two go." Connie says.

"Come on, Patton." I say, leading the way.

"Are you sure?" Patton says, unsure how to handle the tension between us sisters.

"Come on." I urge.

We float out into the street as an old Chevy drives by. The driver does a double take at us but then raises a chubby arm and waves. Some people are taking longer to adjust than others.

"Living people can be so tiresome." I grumble.

"What's happened with you two? Had a fall out?" Patton asks.

I twist a strand of hair as I replay the last few days. Connie's been grumpy, but I don't remember there being a fallout. "I don't think so. She's got a client today and that makes her a bit tetchy sometimes."

"Maybe she's unhappy that we're investigating without her."

"Not just investigating, we've solved the case."

"Hmm." Patton murmurs.

"What?"

"I wonder if we need something stronger, to be able to get Morton to arrest Lovey."

"Stronger than him wiping his fingerprints from the crime scene?"

"I think we should go to his house."

"Are you kidding me? That's the one rule I'd love to break and nobody ever lets me!" I exclaim. What can I say?

I'm nosey. I'd love nothing more than using my dead-ness to go through people's wardrobes. I wouldn't be interested in their mail, or their diaries. I mean, if they left a letter open I might glance at it of course, but it's the clothes I'd like to see. And the make-up! A spray of perfume here and there.

"It's a murder case, I think we could argue that it's a special circumstance. If we got caught, and we're not going to get caught."

"Hold on, are you suggesting we go in without asking Atticus?" I ask.

He nods. "He'll say no. Sometimes it's better to ask forgiveness than permission."

A thrill runs through my body. Finally, the afterlife is getting exciting. "I'm in. Where does he live?"

"Right... about... here." Patton says, turning to the house we're standing in front of with a flourish. It's literally five doors away from Connie's, almost opposite Sheriff Morton's, and I never knew.

"Convenient." I quip. "Is he home?"

"I checked, he's giving one of his riveting talks in the next state. He'll be gone all day."

I nod. The drive's empty, and at the end of the drive stands a neat little bungalow, a swinging chair hanging from the small veranda. Blinds hang at the windows and the brown paint of the clapboard peels in places.

As we approach, it's clear that the house is in disrepair. The cushion of the swinging chair is tinged green with damp, and the veranda itself is supported by wooden beams that creak with the slight wind in the air.

"He's no domestic goddess, I'm guessing." I murmur.

"Shh." Patton says. "Let's go around the back."

The gate at the back opens with a light push, revealing a small, square patch of brown lawn. The back of the house is littered with discarded objects; pots, pans, a sweeping brush, a large empty fish tank, and several bin liners full of rubbish. The stench is awful.

Patton pushes on the back door, but it doesn't open.

"Are we going to -"

"Yep." He says, and disappears through the door.

I groan. The walking through walls thing was a neat party trick when I was first dead, but it costs a fair amount of energy and always seems to mess up my hair. I take a deep breath and close my eyes, knowing that when Patton next sees me, I'll be around 5% less attractive.

When I open my eyes, I'm inside Lovey's house, and Patton isn't even looking at me, which is a result. I plump up my hair and gaze around the room.

"What is this place?" I ask. It's like stepping back in time. A grandfather clock stands in the corner of the room, the ticking of the pendulum inside the waist of the case providing the only noise in the house. The window ledge hosts a series of smaller clocks, all paused on different times. In the corner of the room stands a squeaky-clean jukebox, obviously the focal point of the room, and Patton grins when he notices it.

"Look at this, Sage! It's the Rock-Ola 1454!"

"The what?" I ask.

"Man, you British have no culture. Didn't you have these babies?"

I let out a laugh. My teenage years involved spending as little money as I possibly could, but even on the odd occasion I was taken to a cafe and bought a thick shake by an admiring boy, I'm pretty sure we didn't have these monstrosities in there. "No, I think this is an American thing, for sure."

"You didn't have jukeboxes?"

"Nope. Not in the places I went to."

"Well, I'm sure you were in the coolest places." He says, and his faith in me is touching. I was the coolest person, of course, but then it's not hard to be cool in such an uncool place. There wasn't much competition, if you know what I mean.

"So, Lovey lova da music?" I quip.

"Erm, no, my guess is this baby gets polished and nothing else. Maybe an occasional play to make sure she works." Patton gushes as he stands admiringly in front of the machine.

"She?" I tease.

"Of course!" He says.

"So, it's valuable?"

"I'd say so. Five figures would be my guess."

"Wow." I say. "What about the rest of this old tat? The clocks?"

"Well, the long case clock, definitely. Those things are always in demand. I don't know about these. Hold on, is that -?"

Patton reaches across to the window ledge and picks up one of the objects, and I realise it's not a clock. It's a pink flowered egg, adorned with gold patterning, sitting atop a gold stand.

"What is it?" I ask.

"A Fabergé egg." He says, holding it out to me.

Now, Fabergé eggs I've heard of. But I've never seen one.

It's breathtakingly beautiful, adorned with jewels, and heavy to hold. I return it to the window ledge.

"This place is like a treasure trove." I say. "We'll never find the journal."

6

CONNIE

*J*ill Richardson is a short woman with tight ringlets and all of her bones in the right place. I know because I can see them all, poking through her skin as if they're trying to escape.

I only ever serve water during client meetings but today I'm tempted to lay the table with a full meal to stop the poor woman starving.

"Cake?" I hear myself offer, turning myself into everybody's idea of a stereotypical fat woman.

Jill raises an eyebrow so her supraorbital arch, the bone hiding beneath her eyebrow when it's in its right place, is revealed, sharp and dangerous.

"No." She says, voice clipped. No need for pleasantries with a fat hostess, clearly.

Stop it, I urge myself. I'm being insecure. Thin people can be lovely, too. They don't spend all of their waking hours hating fat people, as I'm sometimes guilty of imagining they do.

"Follow me." I say, and I flash her my biggest smile, hoping it's more friendly than creepy. I don't know what's wrong with me this week. I don't feel like myself, at all. I was hoping that Adele would contact me, suggest I pop over, but I haven't heard a thing from her.

I lead Jill into the consultation room, and guide her to take a seat on one of the two identical couches. I've already prepared the water jug and two glasses, and before I can offer her a glass, Jill is pouring herself one. Got to keep those bones hydrated.

"If I can run through the details? I'll ask you, in a moment, for an item that belonged to the person you want to connect with. I'll use that to call them in, to invite them to join us. They don't have to join us. I can't force a spirit, and I can't offer a refund if they don't turn up."

"Oh, he'll come." She says. That's common, everyone imagines spirits will be beside themselves at the chance of a catch up. Trust me, they're often not. For some people, death is the perfect excuse to not have to put up with an annoying relative's crap any longer.

"Like I say, I'll ask. If the person does come, you can speak to them direct, they'll be able to hear and see you. You might be able to hear or see them." I explain. Now that the whole of Mystic Springs can see spirits, visitors are something of a grey area. Some visitors can see and hear our spirits right away, while other tourists can come for a week and not see a single one.

"Okay, great." She says with a determined nod, then takes a long swig of water and refills her glass.

"Are you nervous?" I ask.

"Nope." She says with a grin. "I can't wait."

"Okay. If you want to give me the item."

"Oh, I don't have an item."

"I need an item to make contact."

"I'm going to sing for him. I know he'll come when he hears me sing."

"Listen, Jill, I can't refund your money if he doesn't come, and using something that belonged to him is the best way to try and avoid wasting your money."

"Mm-hmm." She says, distracted. "I think I'll sing Test To The Goose."

I look at her, blank.

"You've probably heard it. I wrote it myself."

I try to stifle a groan and sit back on the couch. This crazy woman is going to do whatever she wants, I may as well let her. I'm being paid either way.

She rises from the couch and clears her throat, then begins to screech. It's not that her singing is awful, it's that awful would be an improvement. I try to discreetly sit with my head propped up on my arm, so that my hand covers one ear and my hair covers the other.

I'm just about to ask her to stop, because I'm sure all people dead or alive within a 10 mile radius are running away, when a ghostly man appears in the room. He's clearly related to her by blood. He's small and skinny, and his prominent bones give him a drug-addicted look. His cheeks are sallow, his cheekbones high and sharp.

"For Lord sake, make it stop." He curses as he throws himself onto the couch next to me. He sees me watching and holds out an arm, as I reach to shake his hand he pulls it back and waves his hands in the air with a laugh. "Ha! Gets people every time."

"Very funny." I say. "Jill, he's here."

She's getting louder, approaching the climax of the song, and doesn't hear me. I wave frantically across towards her to get her attention.

"He's here!" I shout when she looks at me.

She carries on singing anyway.

"You'll never shut her up. Don't let her start, that's the key."

"And you are?"

"Didn't she tell you? I'm Jack."

"Jack and Jill?" I ask in disbelief. "Let me guess, brother and sister?"

"And we lived up a hill, would you believe. You can't say our parents didn't have a sense of humour, eh?"

Jill screeches her way to the end of the song, holding the last note longer than necessary, then returns to the couch with a satisfied smile. "Told you it'd work, he never could resist my singing. Well, hello Jack."

"Tell her her voice has never sounded more beautiful." He says and descends into laughter that she can't hear.

"He says your voice has never sounded more beautiful."

"Aw, he's a sweetheart. He were always my biggest fan. Right then, shall we get into the details?"

"It's your meeting." I say with a smile.

"I've only got one question really. I can't stop thinking about it, and me and our Jack, we talked about everything."

"You can talk direct to him, he can hear you." I remind her.

"Alright then Jacky-boy, tell me the truth, what were it like? To die?"

The headache doesn't surprise me when it comes the minute I manage to close the door on Jill Richardson, and I pop two tablets immediately. Having to listen to four minutes of her warbling and then an hour of her begging and pleading to talk about death has done nothing to improve my mood.

I plod upstairs to my bedroom and draw the heavy drapes, blocking out the sun. The ceiling fan runs constantly in my room over the summer, and I lie down on top of the covers and close my eyes.

I have nothing else to do today, and rather than reassure me, that thought makes my chest tighten. Nothing to do. A whole day of nothing.

Sure, when I was far too busy, I wished for days filled with nothing but whatever I felt like doing moment by moment. But now I have those days, I'm unsettled.

Grouchy.

I need a hobby, I decide.

I could give dancing a try. I always fancied ball room dancing. The dancers look so elegant, and it's not a style of dance reserved for the slimmer people. I've never had any co-ordination, though, and I can imagine Sage's reaction. She's always said I've got the grace of an elephant.

No, not dancing.

Maybe a gym membership is what I need. But I usually get my gym membership just after Christmas and then cancel the first week of the New Year. I probably shouldn't break that tradition.

Also, a gym membership on its own takes up no time, and I'm not convinced I'm ready for the commitment of actually attending a gym.

I could read more.

Yes, I could definitely read more. Not right now, I realise, as I wince with the pain that runs across my temple.

I have a library card and I don't visit the library anywhere near often enough.

It's the strangest thing. As I think about reading more, I don't feel excited.

And in that moment, I know.

I know what's wrong.

I'm lonely.

No, I miss my sister.

She's taken up with Patton Davey and ditched her sister, that's what's happened. And just like the teenage me, I'm stuck at home wallowing and waiting up for her, while she's having a high old time.

Well, no more.

I'm going to make sure I'm so busy that I don't have time to even remember her name.

That's the plan.

Just as soon as this headache eases.

"Connie!" Adele asks as she opens the door, a baby in her arms.

"Fancy a drink?" I say, holding up the fresh jar of coffee.

"Ah, it's like you're my fairy godmother!" She says. "I literally just ran out. Come in, come in."

Adele's back to her plain appearance, hair tucked behind her ears, slightly stained grey joggers on. I smile.

"Want me to boil the kettle?"

"Sure! There's biscuits in the tin."

"Oh, not for me." I say. "I'm on a bit of a health kick."

"Are you?" She asks in surprise, looking me up and down the way people have to whenever I mention trying to be more healthy. Her gaze stops when it reaches my stomach and she jumps back up to my eyes, gives me a sympathetic smile. "Well, good for you!"

"Well, I just decided right now actually, so it's early days. In the walk from my house to yours, I've managed not to eat a single piece of chocolate, so I'm counting it as a win."

Adele laughs. "As you should. Us chocolate lovers need

all the wins we can get. Throw the biscuits over for me? I haven't got your willpower."

I toss the packet across to her, narrowly avoiding the baby's head. "Oops, you didn't really mean throw, did you?"

She gazes down at the baby and I think about what rubbish it is, her suggesting she's a chocolate lover with no willpower. Even with her post-two-babies body, she's slim, and any wobbly bits will disappear quick enough. Adele's that kind of person. She sets her mind to a goal and achieves it.

"How's Axel?" I ask.

"He's back to his normal, unsleeping self." Adele says.

"Oh that's brilliant. Must be a weight off your minds. Is Taylor back at work?"

"Yep." Adele says.

I go and join her, putting a cup of coffee in front of each of us.

"You're coping okay, while he's at work?" I ask. "I mean, not coping, I know you can cope. I just mean with Axel being poorly."

"It's fine." She says lightly. "I know what you mean. I'm doing fine."

"Taylor too busy with the murder case to chat much?"

"Oh, I don't know. He's pretty distracted lately. I'm sure it's just work pressures."

"It can't be an easy job." I say. "But at least the case has been closed pretty quick."

"Closed?"

"Yeah, they found the murderer, didn't they?" I ask.

"News to me." Adele says with a shrug. The baby in her arms is asleep and she places him down in the bassinet and peeks into the second bassinet, where Scarlett sleeps. I can hear their baby breath, the little dreamy sighs.

"I'm probably wrong."

"Probably." She says, with the directness that you'd expect from the accomplished lawyer she is. "No offence, but I know Taylor wouldn't close such a big case and not tell me. He knows how concerned I am about these murders."

"It's just unlucky." I say, clumsily. "I've been here for years and there was never any trouble. I'm sure things will settle down now."

"I have the babies to think about." She muses. "It's not just me any more."

"You're not thinking of leaving, are you?" I ask, in horror.

She shrugs, rolling her shoulders as she does, and her thoughts transport her, making her unreachable. I sit and drink my coffee in silence, then make an excuse and see myself out. She barely says goodbye.

When I get home, the hard pit still sits in my stomach. A feeling of foreboding.

I'm about to lose the only friend I really have, because some moron killed Emelza Shabley. All over some stupid diary. Who cares whether Mystic Springs was set up by women or a man? Does it really matter?

But it does, I know.

The people of Mystic Springs cling to their heritage, their recent founding, the myth of that band of independent women who set out across the country to find the right place to call home. It's a yearning we can all understand, I think. That desire to set off and leave, walk away from everything we know and start again.

A clean slate.

We cling to the tale of Lavinia Blackbottom the first and her group, not because they're women. That's not it really.

They were spunky, strong, fierce. Everything that media is trying to tell our daughters to be now, these women already were a hundred years ago.

And we can't let go of their epic journey being the truth, without giving up on ourselves.

When I realise all this, I think it's a wonder that only one person killed Emelza Shabley for uncovering that journal. I'm surprised there weren't a hundred local people, all taking it in turns to stick the knife in... literally.

7

SAGE

*T*he front room hosts a single cracked leather chair, a dark wood bureau, and a pile of antique pricing guides that stands nearly as tall as me.

"Let's check the bureau," I suggest.

Patton inspects it then nods and pulls open the doors. The bureau is piled high with papers. Receipts, invoices, pages torn from history books, and stacks of lined paper with hand-scrawled notes.

Edwardian? Circa? one sheet says. That and nothing else.

Another says, *Oct 5, '98 - Gerald rang. Nincumpoop!*

"It's like his whole life is in here." I say, noticing how yellowed some of the papers are. Newspaper clippings almost fall apart at the touch.

"It's all junk." Patton says. "Personal papers, nothing of value. He wouldn't hide the journal here."

"Well, there's nowhere else." I say. We've already searched the modest upstairs; a single bedroom with sparse furniture, a tidy bathroom, and a locked spare room filled with cash registers.

"He might not have hidden it here." Patton says.

"He wouldn't put it anywhere else, surely? That would be risking someone else finding it."

"But leaving it here proves his guilt if the police turn up and search the place."

"It's hopeless, then." I say. "Are you sure it's not in there? Why don't you just pull the whole thing out."

"And get him to report a robbery? Atticus would know it was us. He'd go mad."

"Maybe it's in his car."

"That's a shout. Maybe we should search there next."

"Shh!" I call, at the sound of an engine outside. I peer through the nets. "Lovey's home."

"Crap. He shouldn't be back yet. Maybe he sent all the audience to sleep this time." Patton says. He grabs a bunch of papers from the bureau in one hand, and grabs my arm with the other. "Come on."

We race down the passage and force ourselves through the back door, then float across his garden and through the fence.

By the time Lovey enters the house, we're long gone, but my heart is pounding so loud I wouldn't be surprised if he can hear it from indoors. I hold on to Patton's arm to steady myself.

"That was close." I whisper.

"Not really." Patton says with a grin. "I've had closer."

"You mean you've done that before? Gone in someone's house without permission?"

He taps his nose, won't say another word.

"What papers have you got?"

"I just grabbed what I could. He won't miss a few and who knows, they might be useful. To identify handwriting or something. Come on, let's go and see Morton now."

. . .

Sheriff Morton sits back in his swivel chair, legs raised up on his desk, as he chews the end of a biro.

He doesn't look at all surprised to see us.

"I wondered when you'd come." He says, tone neutral.

"You looked miles away." I say. "Busy?"

His phone vibrates on the desk, the screen lit up to announce an incoming message from *Wife*, and he flips it over, gives us his attention. "Pondering."

"Well, we've been gathering evidence while you've been daydreaming." Patton says, and hands the papers over.

"*Geraldine, 21k*? What evidence is this?" Taylor asks, reading one of the scraps of paper.

"We did an informal search of Lovey Lovegoode's house."

Taylor, new in town, looks blank at the name.

"The local historian. He was desperate to get his hands on the journal that Emelza Shabley found. Made plans to go and see her the evening she was killed."

"Okay, well that's not a crime in itself. Potentially the last person to see her alive? Apart from the killer."

"Maybe." I say. "But that's not all. He went back, the next day, wiped his fingerprints off her waggon."

"You hadn't had the area taped off." Patton says.

Taylor blushes. "My mind's been elsewhere."

"I know. I know about your baby, that's why I didn't report it. But you need to make sure your head is right or hand the case over." Patton says, and I gaze up at him.

Taylor nods slowly.

"It's still not enough." Taylor says. "Let's say he did go over, saw her alive, chatted with her. Then someone else kills her. He could have panicked about seeing her so close to her dying, and that's why he went over to remove his prints."

"It's a possibility." Patton admits. "But he was wiping everywhere. It looks like he'd gone through every cupboard in the waggon. He wouldn't do that as a visitor."

Taylor frowns. "I'll look into it."

"That's it?"

"You've got to leave it alone, you two. It's my job."

"And you're in here, feet up. There's a murderer out there!"

"Fine. I'll question him. But I'll do it in my time, okay. I can't just take your word for everything." Taylor says, and he throws himself up from the chair, grabs his cell phone and car keys. "Is that it?"

"For now." Patton says. "Come on, Sage."

I follow him out, aware that Sheriff Morton is just a few steps behind us, taking the stairs three at a time. He dashes across the parking lot into his car and fires the engine.

"He's in a rush."

"And I don't think he's off to arrest Lovey Lovegoode." Patton says with a grim smile.

"Shame we haven't got a car. I'd be interested in following him." I say.

"He's not worth it." Patton says.

"What shall we do now?" I ask, fluttering spider lashes at him. I'd like to take his mind off the murder case for an afternoon, if he'd let me.

"I need to get some rest." He says. "You should too. Walking through those doors will exhaust us if we don't rest. Let's meet up later?"

"Sure." I say, syrupy sweet smile hiding my disappointment.

Sometimes, life just isn't fair.

. . .

Connie's at the kitchen table when I get home, tapping furiously on the laptop keyboard.

"You're home, then." She says, without taking her eyes off the screen.

"And the winner of Stating The Obvious…"

"Not in the mood." She snaps.

I float over to the laptop to see that she's searching for information about Mystic Springs.

"What are you up to?" I ask.

"I realised, I don't even know the story that well, about how the town was founded. And that's not okay, is it? I should know the roots of the place I call home. Don't you think?"

She's spooking me with this sudden interest in town history, so I just nod.

"Found anything interesting?"

"There's a rumour that the women were gypsies."

"Gypsies?" I say with a gasp. I can imagine Lavinia Blackbottom the fourth's reaction to the suggestion that her great-grandmother was a gypsy.

"It makes sense. A band of women moving around from place to place, I can't believe I haven't thought of it before."

"But where were their husbands? Or was it some female-only gypsy gang?"

"Well, I don't know that. Maybe the husbands stayed behind to work? Or maybe there were no husbands. Maybe it really was a group of independent women."

"I want to believe the last option." I say.

"Do you? You're man mad." Connie scoffs, but there's a lightness in her tone, a softness returning.

"I am, that's true. But in another world, I can imagine it would be nice to be more like you."

"And the punch line?"

"There isn't one." I say. "I'm not joking. You're like those women, aren't you? Strong and independent. I've never even changed a lightbulb without a man helping."

Connie sighs. "It's not all fun my way, you know."

"Well, life never promised anyone to be all fun. But you have a lot to be proud of, moving across here and making a fresh start. You're like the modern day Lavinia Blackbottom the first!"

Connie laughs. "Do you think she was as annoying as her great-granddaughter is?"

"I barely know the woman." I admit. "Is she awful?"

"There's just something about her."

I nearly choke laughing when Connie describes the money coat. "Is she for real?"

"Sadly, I think so."

"Did you find out yet how she's got her money?" I ask.

"I have no idea. She's always campaigning for women's rights but I can't imagine that pays her much, if anything. And she swears she's not living off an inheritance."

"Lottery win?" I joke.

"It could be for all we know." Connie says. "Not that it's anyone's business, but if you walk around in a coat like that, people are going to talk."

The doorbell rings then and Connie stands to her feet, wearily.

"You've had a headache?" I ask, noticing the way she walks slower than normal.

"You noticed." She turns to me and smiles, a smile that shows just how beautiful she is. Her skin is so darn good. She never had acne as a teenager like I did. And then she didn't spend years covering her acne scars with layer on top of layer of foundation, to make it worse.

I cringe when I think back to the days when I'd go to

sleep with a thick coating of cheap foundation on my face, wake up, and apply a second coat on top of the layer from the day before. And my foundation ended, very obviously, with the line of my chin. Teenage girls nowadays are so picture perfect with their contouring and blending compared to the mess I used to apply.

"For you." Connie says, returning to the kitchen and jolting me from my thoughts. In her arms, she holds a huge bouquet of flowers. Roses, stargazer lilies, tulips and lily of the valley in a glass vase. The smell is heavenly.

"Oh wow, who from?!" I ask, giddy with excitement.

"Girl, it's bad enough to always be the deliverer of flowers, I'm not reading the card for you too." Connie says, but she's smiling. "Anyway, three guesses. Who do you think they're from?"

"Patton." I breathe. "They're so beautiful."

I find the card and tear open the envelope.

From your admirer.

"Ooh, the intrigue!" Connie laughs. "That spirit's got it bad."

"You think?" I ask. "I don't think he likes that I'm married."

She rolls her eyes. "Clearly."

I take a deep sniff of the flowers and think back to the way he was so keen for me to return home. He must have been scared I'd miss the delivery. I really do need to learn to stop sulking.

When the doorbell rings out an hour later, I jump up to answer it, expecting Patton.

Sheriff Morton stands on the veranda, freshly shaved, hands in the pockets of his navy slacks. "Can I come in?"

"Sure." I say.

"Is Patton here?"

"No, but I think he's coming soon."

"I'm here." Patton calls, appearing behind Taylor.

"Excuse us for a moment?" I ask, and close Taylor into the house so I can chat to Patton privately.

"Everything okay?" He asks, wide eyed.

"Better than okay!" I gush, and I kiss him on the cheek. "Thank you so much!"

He blinks at me.

"For the flowers! They're beautiful!"

"Oh." He says with a nervous smile. "You like them?"

"They're perfect. I couldn't believe it when they turned up, I was like, I mean, I knew they were for me not Connie of course, but wow... flowers!" I say.

"You deserve them, Sage." He says. His cheeks are flushed and I realise I'm embarrassing him, so I open the door and lead him into the kitchen, where Taylor and Connie stand in silence, both looking at the impressive bouquet.

"You bought these, huh?" Taylor asks Patton. "They look expensive."

"Don't they just." Patton murmurs.

"Erm, we don't need to talk about the price." I say. "Are you here for a social visit?"

"No." Taylor says. "Since you guys are investigating, I thought I'd let you know some news. We might as well work together, you know?"

"Absolutely." I say.

"Fine with me." Patton says.

"Connie?" Taylor asks.

"I just want the murderer caught." Connie says, which is news to me, because last time I checked, she was staying well clear from any investigation. My sister is impossible to understand sometimes.

"Okay, good. I got the lab results back, from the dagger. But also, it's a pretty rare piece, so I was able to trace it. Find out who bought it."

"And?" I ask, eagerly.

"Whoever killer Emelza Shabley wiped their finger-prints afterwards, but the dagger belongs to Lovey Lovegoode."

"I knew it." I say. "That man's house is full of old stuff!"

Connie eyes me.

"We got a special pass to go through his house, for the journal."

"And did you find it?"

"No, but -"

"... he could have hidden it anywhere." Connie finishes my sentence. "Are you going to arrest him, Sheriff?"

"I'm going to call him in for questioning." Taylor says, and I groan.

"Just questioning?"

"The dagger could have been stolen." He says.

"And he didn't report it?" Patton asks.

"Would you? If your dagger was used to kill someone, would you own up to it being yours?" I ask.

"Of course I would." Taylor snaps. "I'm law enforcement, I do the right thing."

"Okay!" I exclaim. "Nobody was questioning your morals!"

"Let's take a minute." Connie says. "We're all on the same side, remember."

"I'm going." Taylor says and stalks out of the house, slamming the front door behind him.

"I said we could work together. I'll never be on the same side as him." Patton says, watching the door.

"What is your issue with him?" I ask.

"He's a womaniser." Patton says, as the oven beeps to signal that Connie's dinner is ready. She puts on an oven glove and opens the door, moving back so the steam can't burn her. She slides an unappetising looking ready meal on to a plate and takes a seat.

"You shouldn't gossip." She chides. "He has a wife."

"I hate gossip." Patton says. "But, I know him of old. I've seen what he's like. He can't run a case when his head's been turned."

"He has been distracted lately." I say.

"His son was ill!" Connie exclaims as she chews a mouthful of the slop.

"Hmm." Patton says, unconvinced. 'I'm going to keep an eye on him."

The police station is in darkness apart from one light in one room, just as it always is after 5pm. As if crime ends after office hours.

Patton and I crouch low in the parking lot, our gaze fixed on the one window that is lit. The only car in the lot belongs to Taylor, so although we didn't see him arrive, we know he's here.

"He could just be working the case." I say, getting restless. We've been watching the window for only fifteen minutes, but it's already lost any novelty the idea of a stake-out might have had. "It's hardly groundbreaking news, is it? Sheriff works late on murder case!"

"Look, go if you want, but I'm staying." Patton says.

I move in closer to him and begin to pick at the grass that erupts from the parking lot in random places.

"Sage, honestly, I'm fine if you want to go home."

"I'll stay, I just don't know what you're hoping to see."

"How about that?" Patton asks.

A car creeps into the parking lot. A green Thunderbird.

"Is that Lovey?" I ask, going by the car's age.

Patton shakes his head, as Lavinia Blackbottom the fourth steps out from the driver's side door. She trots across the parking lot in five-inch heels, a leather mini skirt, and her money coat. The bundles of money dance in the night air as she darts under the cover of the building and pulls out her cell phone.

"I'm here, darling." She crones into the phone.

We watch as other lights flick on within the police station, until the front door is unlocked and Taylor Morton appears. He looks from side to side, not spotting us behind his car, and Lavinia runs into his arms.

"Are they kissing?" I ask.

"Of course they are." Patton spits.

"I'm not sure." I say. "It could just be a hug."

"Yeah, of course. She's come across town to hug the Sheriff..."

The door closes and we watch Sheriff Morton lead Lavinia through the building, turning out each light as they go.

"Wow." I say. "Adele will be gutted."

"I told you he hadn't changed." Patton says, pulling me up from the ground.

"What do we do now?"

"We go. There's nothing else we can do. But at least we know now, his head isn't in the case. We need to run this investigation, Sage. Okay?" He holds my arms and looks at me with urgency.

"Okay." I say.

We head back towards town, both lost in our thoughts. Patton's stewing on Taylor's behaviour, I can tell from his heavy breathing, and I'm thinking about how stupid men are. Sure, his wife's probably not feeling too sexy at the moment after having twins, but she's still leagues ahead of Lavinia Blackbottom the fourth.

8

CONNIE

"*T*hat's not the way it works." I say, as I rinse my breakfast bowl. "For a start, you shouldn't even be here."

"Shall I go out and knock on the front door?" The one-handed spirit in my kitchen asks.

"Please." I say. "I just won't answer."

"Ah, you're spunky. Just how I like them. Gorgeous flowers, by the way."

"They're not mine." I say.

"I'm not surprised. You're not very, well, welcoming to a man."

"Sod off." I say to the spirit who stands before me in my kitchen. He's old, way too old to be sexually attractive, and yet there's something distinguished about him. Something magnetic. "Who are you, anyway?"

"Wilson Bruiser Esq! The pleasure is all yours, I'm sure."

"Wilson Bruiser?" I ask. "It's your journal that's caused all this drama that's going on."

"I've been blamed for some things in my time but never

a murder." He says with a grin, flashing polished white teeth. Obviously false.

"Why would you go and lie, anyway? Pretend you set the town up?"

"I've never told a lie in my life, dear girl." He says, and I think back to that phrase. Something about how the bigger the lie, the easier it is to get people to believe it. Surely, this rogue saying he's never lied is the biggest lie I've ever heard, and yet he's strangely compelling.

"So what exactly do you want from me?"

"I want you to interview me! I know you do appointments. I'll pay."

"Pay me what?"

"I've got a few gold doubloons, fair?"

"Gold doubloons? Are you a pirate now?"

"A pirate?" He asks. "I'm offended. I'm well travelled, that's all. All the rage in Spain, these were. Here, take these and give me an hour of your time."

He sees himself off into the consultation room, leaving me with a handful of gold doubloons. I sigh and follow him.

"Why me? I ask, standing in the doorway, leaning my weight against the doorframe. He's sat down on a couch, flung his legs up on to the coffee table, and even taken his boots off. His toenails are curled over and yellow. "And you're going to have to put your boots back on."

He groans. "Fine. If they're your terms. Come on, let's get on with it. I bet you charge by the minute. I'm not paying for all this flirting."

"I am not flirting with you, trust me!" I exclaim, but I feel my cheeks redden. There's something captivating about him as long as I don't look at his feet.

"In denial. Well, I can feel the sexual tension, but we

really must get the work done first, love. You can have your wicked way with me afterwards, okay?"

I turn away while he struggles, one-handedly, with his boots. There's no way I'm offering to help.

"Tell me when you're done." I call as I gaze out of the window. It's a stifling hot day and I can already feel my underboob area grow damp. Way too hot to be having any sexual tension. Not that I'd want any anyway.

"Are you done?" I ask, and turn around.

Wilson Bruiser sits on my couch, boots back on, but his upper body naked.

"Oh for goodness sake."

"Calm yourself, dear girl. It's just warm in here."

"You're ridiculous." I say, but he's doing it for a reaction. I've seen a torso before. I can ignore it.

I sit across from him and pick up my notebook and pen. "Do you have the questions ready?"

"Me? You're the one doing the interviewing."

"But I don't know how to interview you. And I don't even want to interview you."

"You just want to take me upstairs, don't you, you mucky girl."

I roll my eyes and decide to grit my teeth and get through this as quick as I can. "Name?"

"Wilson Bruiser, I've already told you that."

"Headline of interview?"

"True founder of Mystic Springs breaks century-long silence! Something like that, anyway. You can play around with it."

"So you say you're the true founder of Mystic Springs?"

"I don't say it, it's the truth."

"And your evidence is?"

"The journal."

"The journal's missing."

"Ah." He says, and moves into a prone position on the couch. "That's a problem."

"End of interview then, I guess." I say, jumping up from the couch.

"You give up too easily. I can tell you what it was like?"

"Fine." I say, and I don't really want to ask why I agree. Maybe sitting looking a spirit's naked torso is the most excitement I've had in a while, and I don't feel like admitting that to myself. "Tell me."

"I was wandering the country. Well, the world really, hence the doubloons and all of my accents. A bit of a nomad. I came across Blackbottom - what a name!" He laughs. "She was a frightful character."

"Who was she? There's rumour she was a gypsy."

"Well, of course she was. They all were."

"The women? Were there other men?"

"No, just those poor women." He says. "They were in dreadful need of a man to lead them, and I didn't particularly want the job but there was nobody else around. They were about a day away from dying of dehydration when I found them. They'd set out with a woeful supply of water."

"You just stumbled across them?"

"Well, they stumbled across me." He says. "I was camped out and they all appeared in their waggons. I thought it was a raid, and I was getting ready to take a few prisoners and maybe lose my other hand."

"Hmm." I say, trying to scribble his words on paper.

"Just a bunch of women, scared witless when they saw me. Scared I'd ravish them all, I guess, although within hours they were begging me to, of course."

"Of course." I quip.

"You'll see. I have that effect."

"Carry on." I moan. "You're paying by the minute, remember."

"I rescued them. That's it really. Lead them to water. Let their horses drink. They were lost."

"Lost?"

"Absolutely lost. They'd set out from San Fran, thinking they'd find another plot, and lost all sense of direction. I'll be honest, Connie dear, I couldn't fight them off. It's not good for a woman to be away from men for too long, it does something to their minds. So, they were all well and truly mad. I stepped in and took them under my wing. Said I'd find them a home."

"And?"

"And the rest is history. I lead us to Mystic Springs. It was a gem of a find, with the springs. Nice temperature."

"It was you, not Lavinia?"

"She was with me. I led her, like I led all of them. But it was my discovery, my team of women, and I was the first Mayor. Again, I didn't want to be, but they couldn't lead their horse to water, they had no chance of setting up a new town. I had to be Mayor."

"You?"

"Wilson Bruiser, the man, the myth, the legend. Make sure that gets in the article, okay?"

"You know I'm not a journalist, don't you?"

"What?" He exclaims, sitting bolt upright. "What are you doing, interviewing me then? Taking my doubloons?"

"I'm a medium."

"Oh, for Cripes sake." He says and covers his head in his hands. "I thought they said media. Something in the media. God darn it. Well, you'll have to sell the story to the press."

"You thought I worked in the media?"

"Look, this is fine, it's more authentic this way. Like a

grass-roots movement! Yes, yes, I couldn't have planned this better..."

"Clearly."

"Behave." He says, sparring with me as he strokes his chest hair. I look away.

"I need some more details about the town being set up, to make it believable." I say.

"Okay, what do you want to know?"

"Why the name?"

"Oh, I left that to the women. Women are good with little tasks like that. Makes them feel important. I gave them guidance, of course. Said the name had to have the same number of letters as my name. Wilson Bruiser. Mystic Springs."

"What was it like being Mayor?"

"Hell." He says with a groan. "Women shouldn't be in gangs like that. There were days I was tempted to chop my other hand off, just to shock them into being quiet. They argued over everything, especially who was spending the most time with me. Such jealousy."

"And what was Lavinia's role? Because everyone believes she was the leader, and the Mayor."

"She was a power-hungry little cow." He seethes. "Always calling meetings and trying to show me up. She was wild. She'd fight me like she was a man! Throwing little punches, bless her. And then she'd calm down and be all apologetic. I think she liked the kissing and making up, you know. She weren't bad in the sack, I admit that."

"You really are insufferable. I can see why she'd throw punches at you." I say.

He lets out a sharp laugh. "Word spread about our little home, and more and more people came. It was an exciting time! People moving out of the cities, wanting to be part of a new adventure. We had to pretend the women weren't gypsies, of course. Hide the waggons. Nobody wanted to join a gypsy camp."

"Why not?"

"Well, they're thieves, aren't they?"

"Is there any group of people you can't offend?" I ask, incredulous. I was mad to consider him attractive.

"Not that I can think of, why, have I forgotten one?" He asks, flashing the white teeth again. "Although you English are fine chaps."

"Right, that's enough for an article. I'll see what I can do." I say, although I'm pretty sure I'm throwing the notes in the trash as soon as he leaves. "You can go now."

"You're as warm as an icicle."

"That's the goal." I say.

"As welcoming as a Do Not Enter sign."

"Very funny."

"As friendly as a smack in the face!" He exclaims, awaiting my reaction.

"You can see yourself out." I flash him a smirk and begin to walk out of the room.

"You're as spunky as your sister."

"You know Sage?" I ask, the smirk well and truly gone.

"Oh yes." He says. "I hope she likes the flowers I sent."

The newspaper run an article about Wilson Bruiser the very next day, but it's nothing to do with me.

It seems that Emelza Shabley sent excerpts from the journal to the press before she was killed. The date mark on the envelope was the day before her demise.

"Good news day!" Ling cries, alone again at the news stand.

"This Wilson Bruiser's a real piece of work." I mutter.

"Handsome, though." She says with a grin. "Don't tell my husband."

"Where is he, Ling? Does he ever do any work?"

She shrugs. "The man useless."

I shake my head. No young women grow up dreaming of getting married to a husband like Ling's, who lies in bed while they go out to work. I wonder why she stays with him.

"Big news for town, yeah?" She asks.

"I guess." I say, still not wanting to believe that a man as arrogant and pig-headed as Wilson Bruiser could really have founded the town.

As I walk back across town towards home, I spot Lavinia Blackbottom leaving the police station.

From the clothes she's wearing, I wonder if she's been arrested for being out in a state of undress.

She waves at me when she sees me, as if we're friends.

"Connie, dear!" She calls.

I walk across to her.

"Yes?"

"Just wanted to say hi! Hi!"

"Erm... hi." I say. "Are you okay?"

"Oh yes, I've been helping Sheriff Morton with his enquiries. This whole business is so stressful. It's what's wrong with our country, you know. You can't achieve anything without someone wanting to come along and take it. Well, we'll get to the bottom of who hurt poor Emelza."

"I thought you didn't get on with her?"

"She had a dishonest streak, can hardly be blamed given her background."

"That she was a gypsy, you mean?"

"Exactly. You've heard the rumours, too? Poor girl didn't deserve to die, though."

"Well..." I say, lost for words.

"Nice chatting!" Lavinia says, and totters across the empty parking lot in the direction of her home.

The police station front door opens and Sheriff Morton appears in the doorway. "Connie? Can I have a word?"

"Sure." I say.

He leads me through the building, up the stairs to the first floor, and past an open plan area with eight empty desks.

"Is this the HQ?" I ask, looking at the mess on top of seven of the desks. The last one, if used at all, must be used by someone obsessive about tidiness. It must drive them mad working with such messy people, I think.

"It would be if we had any resources." He says with a high. "It's mainly just me."

"Surely one Sheriff can't solve a murder case on his own?"

"Well, I'm not on my own, am I? You're still helping, right?"

I nod, although I'm not sure I want to be involved. I've realised that if two murders make Adele want to leave town, she doesn't care whether the case is solved or not. She just wants to leave, and keep her babies safe. I can't criticise her for that, as much as I don't want my new friend to go.

"What's on your mind?" He pokes as we reach his office. It's a small cubicle, fit out with a flatpack desk and a computer that whirs in protest against having to work. I look out of the window over the main road just as an old Thunderbird goes past.

"Wilson Bruiser came to see me." I say.

"And?"

"Well, he's horrible."

"Could he have done it?"

"Done what?" I ask, clueless.

Taylor glances at his cell phone and sighs. "Killed Emelza."

"Oh God." I say, and a chill runs through my bones. Why hadn't it occurred to me? I think of how vile he was. How much he seemed to hate women, and gypsy women especially. And he was no stranger to violence, if the stump at the end of one of his arms was anything to go by.

Taylor looks at me curiously.

"Yes." I say. "I think he could have."

"Great." Taylor says sarcastically. "Just when I'm starting to think this case is straightforward, now we have two suspects."

"Have you spoken to Lovey Lovegoode yet?"

"I'm working on it." He says, with another glance at the cell.

"Is everything okay, Taylor?" I ask, thinking of Patton's words.

"It's just a stressful case." He says, arms folded, as he gazes out across the street.

"You look like you're waiting for a call?"

"Always." He grunts.

The gypsy women are awful beasts, determined to take my treasure, my time and my mind.

I fight them off best I can but I'm only a man. I have my limits.

One woman, Lavinia Blackbottom, is the worst. My mortal enemy, more feared than any manly foe I came across. The men fight fair. She would seduce me into bed and then stab a knife in my back.

"Unfortunate wording, isn't it." Adele says. We're dining out for the night, at my suggestion, while Taylor holds the babies, and so far it's been 26 minutes since we ordered and no sign of our appetizers.

"Stabbing a knife in the back?" I say. The newspaper was on the table when we got here, I swear. I'm not that much of a geek that I'd bring my newspaper out with me to read across the dinner table.

"He obviously thought he'd get to it before anyone could read it, apart from Emelza." Adele says with a shrug.

The waiter dashes past our table, a harried man with a balding head. A crash comes from the kitchen, followed by shouting.

"Shall we just go?" Adele asks.

"No way! This is your night of freedom, we're going to stick it out to the bitter end." I say, and she flashes me a weak smile.

"I don't know how nachos can take half an hour to prepare."

"Maybe they're really good nachos." I tease.

"I doubt it." She says as the waiter reappears, cheeks red, and walks past us and straight out of the restaurant.

"Erm, I think he just left."

"Ugh, we should go, come on." She says.

"Too late." I say as an overweight man with a beard that touches his belly button appears from the kitchen, holding a plate of food as if it's an Olympic medal he's just won.

"And good evening ladies, here we got the nachos. Enjoy!" He places the plate down in front of us with a flourish, takes a small bow which puts his beard hair scarily close to our food, and returns to the kitchen.

Adele and I look at each other and burst into laughter.

Our dish holds a small portion of tortilla chips with some grated cheese sprinkled on.

"They haven't even melted the cheese." Adele exclaims in between laughter.

"Maybe we should call it a night, after all." I say, and with that, I pull out a ten dollar bill from my purse, and we dash out of the restaurant and into the sticky night air.

9

SAGE

"What time do you call this?" I ask as Connie comes stumbling through the door in a ball of laughter. She trips up the front step and almost lands on her behind in the hall.

"Sorry mum!" She cries, which sends her deeper into her laughter.

I shake my head because this is not the way our relationship goes. I'm the fun one who arrives home at all times and laughs it off. And I am definitely *not* her mum.

"I'm going to sleep." I say and float upstairs. She can explain herself in the morning.

When I wake up, I can smell the bacon and hear the banging around in the cupboards.

How predictable. Connie needs grease to soak up a hangover.

I'm almost impressed with this sudden wild-child behaviour.

As I go into the kitchen, however, it's clear that Connie isn't the one cooking.

"What are you doing here?" I ask.

Wilson Bruiser turns from the frying pan and grins at me, pearly whites twinkling.

"I thought I owed you breakfast after the wild time you showed me last night."

I wrinkle my nose. "Do I look like I have a memory problem? In your dreams, Bruiser."

"Those too." He quips and cracks an egg into the pan.

"Seriously, you can't be here. We have a rule. You need permission to come in a person's house."

"Oh, I was invited. Begged, practically, by your lovely sister."

"I doubt that very much." I say. *Where is she, anyway?* She never sleeps in.

"Mushrooms?" He offers.

"Bruiser, I'm a spirit, I can't eat."

"No wonder you have that lovely, trim figure. I love the smell, I do. Takes me back to my campfire days, cooking does. Nothing like a good meal when you're sleeping under the stars."

"You should have stayed outside to get the full experience." I say. "I'm going to find Connie."

"Don't disturb her, she had a big night." He says with a wink.

I roll my eyes and return upstairs. Life is becoming surreal.

Connie's in her bed, still fully dressed, her pillow wet with drool.

"Wake up!" I say, a little louder than necessary. I'm normally the one being woken up after a fun night, the novelty of being in the other position has gone to my head, I guess. She jolts upright, eyes tiny, curly hair matted to the side of her face.

"What's wrong?" She slurs.

"Are you still drunk?" I ask, arms folded, enjoying being the pious one who went to bed early for once.

"Drunk? I didn't have a single drink."

"Well, you can explain all of that later. There's a strange man in your kitchen cooking breakfast."

She groans. "Do you mean Patton?"

My ghostly face drains of colour. Patton. He'll be over shortly. No way can he find Wilson Bruiser at my home knocking up breakfast. I cover my face with my hands, just as the doorbell rings.

"That'll be Patton." I say, and float out of Connie's room. It stinks like a hangover in there, regardless of what she says.

"Then who?" She calls after me.

"Wilson Bruiser." I shout to her. "You need to get ready and come down."

By the time I get downstairs, Wilson has, to my horror, opened the door. He's wearing Connie's Kiss Me Quick apron over his own ghostly clothes, and has only opened the door a fraction.

I go to his side and see Patton, dejected, on the veranda.

"Ah, here she is." Wilson is, and he slides an arm around my shoulder. "We had a big night, if you know what I mean. Need some protein!"

Patton blinks and looks down. "I'll leave you to it."

"Good idea, old pal." Wilson says, already moving to close the door.

"Oh, stop it. Come in, Patton. Wilson's talking rubbish as normal." I say with a glare in the old man's direction. "On second thoughts, I'll come out to you."

I close the door after me and stand with Patton, who can't meet my gaze.

"How did he get in?"

"I don't know." I say, and even as I say it I'm aware of what a weak lie it sounds like. "Look, I had nothing to do with it. The man's a creep. I woke up, smelt the bacon cooking and thought it would be Connie down there."

"Where is Connie?"

I roll my eyes. "She was out late last night and, trust me, she's not a pretty sight this morning."

Patton begins to smile. "You sound like her mom."

"I do not!" I argue. "Why does everyone keep saying that?!"

The front door opens. Connie appears, a hand protecting her eyes from the sun.

"Geeze, you look like..."

"Not now." She snaps, and steps in closer to me and Patton. She drops her voice. "Listen, we have to get rid of him. He's a suspect."

"I thought..."

"Think about it. It's his journal. And the bits that have been leaked to the press talk about killing with a knife in the back."

"But the knife was Lovey's."

"And Wilson clearly goes wherever he wants, without being asked. He's trying to frame Lovey."

I groan. This investigation is turning out to be a whole lot of trouble.

"Let's kick him out."

"I've got a better idea." Connie whispers. "He loves to talk. Let's try and trip him up into confessing."

I glance at Patton, to check that he thinks that idea is as nuts as I do, but he's grinning.

"Let's do it." He says.

Nobody even asks me what I think, which is worrying as I seem to be the only one thinking straight lately.

Getting Wilson to talk is as easy as anyone would guess.

"If you're trying to fill in the blanks, my dear, last night was even better than you remember." He says as he presents Connie with a huge mound of bacon and eggs. No mushrooms in sight.

"You're a hoot." Connie says, eyeing the food carefully.

"It's not poisoned." Wilson says. "I thought you women wanted a modern man like me, a man who'd ravish you *and* also cook you breakfast?"

"What are you doing here?" I ask. Typical man, he's out of the kitchen without making an attempt to clean up the mess he's made. The kitchen looks like it's been used to prepare a seven-course meal for a hundred people, the number of pans Wilson has managed to use.

"I'm being sociable." He says. "You're awfully grumpy with me, to say I bought you flowers."

"Ha, nice try. Patton bought me those flowers." I say.

Patton shifts in his seat.

"Ah, taking the credit for another man's romantic gestures, are you?" Wilson asks, and Patton holds his head in his hands.

"Patton?" I ask. "You told me -"

"You put me on the spot." He says, not looking at me. "I didn't want to disappoint you."

"Wow." I say. "So, you're my admirer, really?"

"You can thank me later. Upstairs." Wilson says with a wink.

"Let's stay focused. There's more important things to talk

about." Connie snaps. "Wilson, you obviously appeared here to get your journal back? Have you done that now?"

"What?" He asks, waving his arm stump around as if he's acting out a sword fight. "Why would I want a battered old journal?"

"Well you did only turn up when word got out about it."

"That's true, but just because two things happen at the same time doesn't mean they're related. Do you know the difference between causation and correlation?"

"What?" I scoff. No way is this man trying to lecture us.

"Causation and correlation. Causation is -"

"No, we know that." I say. The scent of bacon is rich in the air and it's making me feel a bit queasy. Connie hasn't eaten anything.

"So, the two things aren't connected."

"Why are you here, then?"

"For the publicity." He says, still fencing with the air. "People are talking about me, I'm the man of the hour it seems. It would be churlish to ignore my public, don't ya think honey?"

"You've got no interest in your journal? It'll be worth some money, if it's real."

"Of course it's real, silly. I wrote it with my own hand."

"Don't have to ask which one, do we?" Patton says with a smirk.

"The same one I used to choose flowers with, mutton head!" Wilson exclaims as his body stills. "It's spirits like you who give the rest of us a bad name. No wonder they want us gone!"

"What are you talking about now?" Connie asks.

"The petition. There's a meeting in the town hall any time now."

"A meeting about what?" I ask. The man, the myth, the legend is full of crap.

"About banishing spirits, of course! The town has decided you're a menace!"

"Hold on. That's why you're here! You're distracting us!"

"Distracting you from your civic duty... would I do such a thing? Anyway, is that the time? Must dash! Got a hot date with a spook I used to know..." He sing-songs and, with that, he disappears.

"Ugh!" I cry. "That spirit infuriates me! He *should* be banished!"

"He's probably making it up. Why would the town want to get rid of spirits?"

I think back to the way some locals have looked at me since they were given the ability to see the dead. I can believe that some would rather have things go back to how they were.

"If the town think the spirits are dangerous, they'll want you gone." Connie says. She's alert now, eyes wide, posture straight. "Come on, we need to check it out."

The Mystic Springs Town Hall is in darkness, the doors not just closed but locked.

Connie bangs on the heavy door until, finally, a tiny old woman answers.

"Yes?"

"Doris, let us in." Connie says, pushing her way in. We follow, and I stick my tongue out to the old bat who watches me aghast.

In the hall itself, a small group of people are gathered around in a circle, not one of them a day under seventy-five.

The leader of the group appears to be a small, mole-like woman who holds a clipboard.

"All in favour -" She is in the middle of saying when she notices our group storming towards her.

"What the hell is happening here?" Connie asks.

"It's a meeting."

"A meeting about what?"

Mole-woman pushes her glasses up her nose and reads from the clipboard. "Meeting to discuss banishing spirits from Mystic Springs. We were just about to take the vote."

I look around the group. It's a gathering of the town's most miserable people, that much is clear. And all of them are anti-spirits.

"I didn't get an invitation." Connie says.

"Oh, really, dear?" Mole-woman says. "The postal service isn't what it used to be."

"This is rubbish. You've clearly only told the people who will vote the way you want it to go."

"That's a very strong accusation to make." Mole-woman says, but she's a paper warrior, a letter writer, a complainer with perfect grammar. She isn't built for face-to-face confrontation.

"You know that this is wrong. Adjourn the meeting until tomorrow. Give everyone a chance to come and vote." Connie urges.

"Well, we're already taking the vote..." The woman mumbles. Her group are silent. Any support she might have hoped for from them isn't appearing.

"Sage, Patton, go and round up as many people as you can. Now!" Connie orders, and we're on the move before she's even finished.

"I suppose we should give them a few minutes." One of the group says.

"I didn't realise there'd been postal problems. I just thought nobody else cared." Another says.

Mole-woman develops a nervous twitch.

Out in the street, we scream at whoever we see - spirits especially - that they need to get to the town hall urgently. I don't know if you live in a small town, but here, people are desperate for a piece of gossip, so they immediately drop whatever they were in the middle of, and race across to the hall.

When we've sent around thirty spirits in that direction - all of whom we're fairly confident won't want to be banished - we decide it's safe to head back to the hall ourselves. Mole-woman didn't have that many in her circle.

"Why do you even want to banish the spirits?" Connie is asking when we float back into the Town Hall. We leave the doors wide open so more people can follow us in.

Mole-woman has dropped her clipboard and is in the corner of the room, whispering into a historic brick of a cell phone.

I rush to Connie's side. The circle of mole-followers aren't answering her. They seem stunned by the whole situation but I'm darn sure they're drafting complaint letters in their heads to send after this is done.

"Think we got enough?" I ask her.

She does a quick head count, her own head bobbing with each person. She nods at me, and clears her throat.

"Can we get this meeting back in motion?" She calls across to mole-woman, who freezes, gives one final whisper into the cell phone and returns to her seat.

"This is a meeting to -" She begins, reading again from the clipboard.

"Why do you want to banish spirits?" Connie asks, her gaze focused on mole-woman. The right corner of mole-woman's mouth is twitching so much I worry for a moment she might be having a stroke.

"It's alright, dear, she always does that when she's nervous." An old man from the circle says to me with a wink after noticing the alarm on my face. I flutter my eyelashes at him, thinking a little attention from a hot spirit like me might help him vote in the right way.

"They're a menace." She says, her voice dancing with nerves. "A spirit killed poor Emelza Shabley."

"How do you know that?"

"Mark my words, it's a spirit!" She says, as if that's that, case closed. The mole has spoken.

"Let's just get to the vote, you can't talk sense into some people." I say, giving a conspiratorial wink to my new old man friend.

"All those in favour of banishing spirits from Mystic Springs, please raise your hand now." Mole-woman warbles. She raises her own hand, surprise surprise.

In total, she has the support of four other people, all of them as ancient as her, and at least two of them appearing to be so deaf I'd hazard a guess they have no idea what they're voting for. My man friend keeps his arm down. See, I've still got it.

"Ahem." She says, carefully counting the votes and writing a large 5 on her paper. "And all those in favour of not banishing spirits from Mystic Springs, please raise your hand now."

Forty-two hands go up, including the hand of one of the deaf men, who I'm now starting to think might imagine the arm-raising as some kind of geriatric aerobics class. He probably thinks he's done the advanced version by raising his arm twice.

I keep a sharp eye on mole-woman as she counts the hands and scratches a shaky 42 into her paper.

"That's that, then." Connie says. "And make sure that in future, no meetings like this are called without everyone being informed. You know the rules."

Mole-woman drains of colour at this direct a confrontation, and keeps her gaze straight ahead, pretending it isn't happening.

"Meeting dismissed." She says, and the group of old relics attempt to get up out of their seats.

"We did it!" I say with a grin, but Connie is serious.

"This is bad news, Sage." Connie says. "We don't want to lose public support."

"Well, we obviously haven't, we won."

"This time we did." She says, thoughtfully, as we leave the Town Hall.

"Excuse me!" A voice calls after us. We stop in our tracks, to see the old man I spoke to inside, walking after us. To my surprise, despite his age, he's sprightly on his feet, and smartly dressed in a shirt, jacket and bow tie. He sports a neat, close-cropped white beard, and his face is so riddled with liver spots that he appears tanned.

"Thanks for your support in there." I say with a smile.

"My pleasure. I was always going to vote that way." He says with a charming smile. He holds out his hand, first to me, then to Connie, and bends slightly to kiss hers. "Finian Archbold. I wanted to say how spectacular you were in there."

"Oh. Thanks." Connie says, looking at me. I shrug.

"We couldn't give up without a fight." I say. I'm clearly going to have to handle the conversation.

"Well, I'm glad you didn't. The spooks keep things interesting around here! I have a few at home, but then what would you expect, living in a castle!" He says with a laugh.

"Hold on." I say. There's only one castle nearby. "I know who you are now. You live at Mystic Castle?"

He nods.

"You had it built from your own design, didn't you? I'm sure I read about it."

He laughs. "I made some rudimentary drawings, the professionals took it from there."

Mystic Castle sits on a bluff just outside the town, and the rumours I've heard say that the owner - Finian himself - lived in a motor home on site throughout the decade it took to build.

"It looks amazing." Connie says. She's always loved castles.

"Come on over." Finian suggests.

"Erm..." Connie says. "I'm not feeling too great right now."

"She had a heavy night." I say with an eye roll. "I'd love to come and see it."

"Well, great. How about you go and rest your head, and come across this afternoon?" He offers. There's something mischievous about him, and I find myself intrigued by him. Maybe I am man mad. It seems every time Patton's back is turned, I'm chatting to a new man. Or an old man, in many cases. But I'm single, I remind myself. Patton might be sniffing around, but he hasn't asked me out.

"We'd love to." I say impulsively, ignoring the glare I can feel Connie directing at me.

10

CONNIE

*W*hy we need to go and see a rich eccentric's imitation castle, I have no idea. It's not as if Sage has ever been a history buff. That's me, and I like the real thing, not the flashy fakes that money can buy.

"What's wrong with you?" She asks as she follows me back home. All I want to do is lie in a darkened room. In silence.

"You very nearly got banished, Sage, don't you understand that?"

"Well, of course I do. I was right there with you. But we didn't get banished. We won. Let's celebrate."

"There's nothing to celebrate, Sage." I say as we reach the veranda. "I'm going to get some rest, don't wake me up. My head's banging."

"Fine." She says, and while I come into the house, she stays out on the veranda to sulk.

When I wake up a few hours later, my head's clear and my heart is heavy.

I've been such a grouch.

I get out of bed and make it, tossing all of the pillows on the floor and then smoothing my comforter across the whole of the surface, before arranging the pillows neatly. Something about a freshly made bed is so soothing for the soul. I stand back and admire my work. A job well done.

"For God's sake." I say aloud. Have I really become a woman who prides herself on a neat bed? I purposely untuck one of the corners and ruffle it so it looks messy, then nod with satisfaction.

I sigh.

I know what I need to do.

I find Sage out on the veranda still, gliding back and forth on the rocker. She doesn't look at me, and I can't blame her.

"I'm sorry." I say, and that gets her attention. "I know I've been a real grump lately."

"Mm-hmm." She agrees. Gotta love the brutal honesty only a sister can give you.

"I don't think all this free time is good for me." I say, plopping myself down on the decking beside her.

"Oh, really?" She asks sarcastically, raising an eyebrow in my direction. "Let me guess, you need a new hobby."

"Well." I say, taking a breath. "I was thinking, if you'd have me, I'll help you investigate Emelza's murder."

Sage smiles at me and nods. "Of course I'll have you."

"You're sure I won't cramp your style with Patton?"

"No chance." She says quickly. Who says that death can't change a person? I'd never have got that answer out of her when she was alive and chasing a different boy every week.

"So, you wanna go see this castle?"

She grins and claps her hands together with glee, like a small child. "Yes!"

"Come on then." I say. "I think we should be careful of this guy, though, I've heard some weird things about him."

"Oh, that's strange. I thought someone who had their own castle built would just be a regular joe."

"Oh, ha ha." I say, but the mood is good-natured and we fall into a comfortable chatter as we walk through town. Nettie Frasier is out in her garden, a large straw hat protecting her head from the heat. She gives us a small wave then returns her attention to her borders, secateurs in hand.

"She's so darn beautiful." Sage says wistfully as we pass.

"So are you." I say, the compliment slipping out with none of the sarcasm we usually reserve for each other. She turns to me and smiles.

Wilson Bruiser sits on a bench across the street, and without saying a word, we both speed up to get past him without him noticing. He doesn't even look up, his attention focused on the ground. He may even be asleep.

"What's the deal with him?" I ask. "You like him?"

"No!" She exclaims, a little too strongly.

"But he sent you flowers."

"I think that implies he likes me, not the other way around." She says, which is a good point. "And I'm pretty sure that guy has a regular order at the florist for a different girl each week."

"Hmm." I say, thoughtfully.

"What?"

"I know you, Sage. I know when someone's got your attention."

"He's a suspect, you said." She says. "I try not to date murderers."

"Don't we all." I quip, as we approach the bluff. Mystic Castle stands proudly atop the crest, a gothic design headed with needle spires. Despite being only a few years old, it's finished to appear as if it's sat, like a guardian, on the bluff for centuries. It gives me the spooks.

"How do you get in a castle, anyway?" I ask, chatting to try and hide my nerves. "Is there a doorbell?"

Sage is so busy gazing up at the structure that she doesn't answer me, if she even hears me.

The door is enormous, big enough to get an Army out of, which I guess may be the intention although it's hard to imagine that Mystic Springs would ever need defending. Within the huge door, though, is a regular sized door, and as we approach, that smaller door opens.

Finian Archbold greets us with drinks of cranberry juice served in goblets, and I decide to relax and enjoy the theatre of it all. Sage, of course, can't drink hers, but she carries the goblet with her, apparently reaching the same decision as me. It's not every day you get to go inside a gothic castle, even if it is an imitation.

"This place is incredible." Sage breathes as she gazes at the flying buttresses above our heads.

"It's so authentic." I admit, somewhat reluctantly. "Is it based on one place?"

"I took inspiration from several places." Finian says as he leads us into a large banquet hall, slipping comfortably into the role of tour guide. "Prague Castle is perhaps the closest, with a touch of the Papal Palace. You say you want to build a gothic castle and people imagine it's going to be an imitation of Hunyad - Dracula's castle, you know? - so I steered away from that. And it was important to me that it be very modern."

"Modern?" I repeat.

"Oh, yes. Watch this." He says, and an infectious grin appears on his face. "Lights, on!"

Hidden in the recesses of the ceilings are dozens of tiny circular lights, which all flutter on at his command.

"Wow." I exclaim.

"Pretty cool, isn't it?"

"This must have cost an insane amount of money. Am I allowed to ask what you do?" Sage asks.

She's obsessed with knowing how wealthy people have earnt their money, and normally I'd tell her not to be so rude, but I'm desperate to know myself, so I stand back and hope he answers.

He chuckles. "I was an oil baron."

"Oh." Sage says.

"Were you hoping I made my money playing online poker, or something?" He asks with a good-natured laugh. "I'm far too dull for that. My grandparents made money in oil and the men of the family have stayed in the industry. I made a ridiculous amount of money and got out before I was 50."

"Did you always want to have your own castle?"

"Since I was a boy." He says. "We were fairly well-travelled and I have great memories of Prague Castle in particular. I'd explore the grounds alone, I was always much more interested in the outside. I used to gaze up at the castle and try to imagine what it would be like to see that sight and call it home."

"And is it as good as you imagined?" I ask.

He grins, and I can see the boy he must have been then. "It's even better!"

A cold blast shoots through us then and I feel myself shiver.

"Dolores, come and say hi." He says, glancing around. "She's awfully shy."

He gives the spirit a moment to show herself but the warmth has returned, she's clearly long gone.

He shrugs. "She keeps herself to herself. It's Tobias you need to watch, he's a bit of an attention seeker with guests. He'd be all over you."

"Oh, they all are." Sage says with a high laugh.

"So, you were always going to vote to keep the spirits, since you let some live with you?" I ask.

"Absolutely."

"Then how did you get invited?"

"Oh, I wasn't invited." He says. "I was just passing, on my way to see Lavinia. I saw that old woman - the one with the twitch - sneaking people into the town hall and thought it didn't seem right, so invited myself along. I think she looked at my age and assumed I'd agree with the rest of them."

"You know Lavinia?"

"Oh yes. Doesn't everyone know Lavinia?"

"What do you think to these rumours that the town was founded by a man?" I ask.

He takes a deep breath. "It's a dreadful business, really. Makes me glad I'm up here out of the way. You want dinner? The chef's here."

"You have a chef?" I ask in disbelief.

"Of course!" He grins. "I never took a wife and I never learnt to cook, so I didn't have much of a choice there."

I shake my head. This is too surreal. "We have time?"

"I do." Sage says. Her eyes are everywhere.

"Come on, follow me." He leads us into a second banquet hall, this one more intimate. The table is laid for six, as if company is always expected, and Sage and I take seats next to each other.

"You eat everything?" He asks me, and I choose to not take the comment as a commentary of my size.

"I do." I admit.

"Let me speak to the chef. Chat among yourselves, I won't be long."

He leaves us alone and Sage and I turn to each other, both too stunned to know where to begin. As I look at her, my attention is drawn to a huge oil painting that hangs above the fireplace.

"Oh my God, is that -?" I begin, pointing to the art piece. On it, a naked woman lies across a chaise lounge, and although she isn't looking towards us, I'm sure I recognise her.

"It's Lavinia." Sage confirms, and we both get up from our seats and move closer. "Well, isn't she a dark horse."

"The artist has flattered her." I say and immediately regret the words. Lavinia's had a good figure for as long as I've known her, but this portrait takes years off her. Either that, or Lavinia and Finian go way back.

"Ah, you found my muse." Finian says as he reappears in the room. He joins us and admires the artwork, and I suddenly feel uncomfortable that we're all here admiring Lavinia's naked form without her knowing.

"I'm sorry." I stutter. "We shouldn't have -"

"You should have! It's out here to be admired. Isn't it beautiful?"

"It's, erm, nice." I say. "I didn't realise the two of you were -"

"Were what?" He asks.

I stare at him, unable to finish the sentence.

"She means, she didn't know the two of you were bonking."

"Bonking? Ha! You English are adorable." He says and descends into a fit of laughter. "No way! None of that!"

"Oh." I say, confused. I can't imagine any of my friends

wanting a naked painting of me above their dining table, unless it was to put them off eating.

"Just friends." He says. "Although there may have been a bit of slap and tickle here and there. Anyway, the chef's preparing a gothic speciality. Sheep's brains!"

The colour drains from my face. I'd imagined, with all of the modern touches throughout this castle, that the food would be modern too.

"Ooh!" He exclaims with a grin. "I got you good! You should have seen your face! Hilarious!"

Sage begins to laugh as well, but my stomach is still churning.

"She's making steak and salad." He says between his laughter.

Sage grins. "He got you good."

I shake my head and cast a warning look at her. Her head's turned more often than my mattress.

"I wish I could still eat." Sage says. "What I wouldn't do for steak and salad."

"Sheep's brains! You really believed me, didn't you!" Finian chokes, as the chef appears with two plates of rare steaks and exotic looking salads. I can see the blood under the meat before she places them on the table. I've lost my appetite.

I can see him on the bench as we approach, still slumped in the same position as earlier.

Sage instinctively moves to cross the road again, but I don't follow her.

"I'm going to talk to him." I say. "You go home, find Patton. Hmm, probably get Sheriff Morton too. We'll have a meeting when I get back."

"You'll be okay?" Sage asks, gazing towards Wilson. I need to keep the two of them apart. Whether or not he's a murderer, he's not the spirit for her.

"Absolutely. I won't be long."

I approach Wilson slowly, trying to plan what I'm going to say to him, and then decide that the natural, unrehearsed way is better.

He's asleep. I can hear snoring from thirty feet away.

I plop myself down on the bench next to him. Across the road is Nettie's house, so it doesn't take three guesses to work out why he's parked himself here. As Sage herself said, Nettie is beautiful. She's also way out of Wilson's league.

"Wake up." I say quietly, knowing as I do it that startling a suspected murderer is perhaps not my best idea.

He wakes slowly, groggily, and emits a loud noise from his rear end before he notices me.

"Better out than in!" He says in an English accent. "To what do I owe this pleasure?"

"It's not a pleasure, I'm afraid." I say. "There are some dreadful rumours going around town about you, Wilson. I thought you should know."

"Do tell, dear girl." He says, eyes wide with mock interest. The man is infuriating.

"Rumour has it that you killed Emelza Shabley." I say, and wait. He gives no reaction at all for ten seconds, and then lets out a long yawn, his open mouth revealing his bright pearly whites and foul breath.

"All for that tatty old diary?"

I shrug. "It makes sense in a way. You turned up when the diary was discovered. Why wouldn't you want to have it back, it is yours. It's understandable."

"No." He says with a quick shake of his head. "You have it all wrong. I'm the person who wants that darn thing least.

I know what it says because I wrote it! It means nothing to me now."

"You could sell it."

"I don't need money."

"Those flowers don't pay for themselves." I say with raised eyebrows.

He grins. "No money needed."

"Oh, Wilson. You didn't steal them?"

"I'd call it creative licensing. Sneak into the florist after dark, grab one of the pre-arranged selections, write out the card and add it to the pile going on the van the next morning."

"Wow." I say. "You really are unbelievable."

"Thanks, darlin'." He says, transforming his accent again. "So, as you can see, I got no reason to want that diary. And certainly not enough reason to go killin' anyone."

"Well, that doesn't matter much." I say, attempting my best pitiful voice. "The Sheriff needs a person to blame and he's picked you."

"Ha! Is that the way justice works here now? It wasn't like that in my day."

"In your day there were no murders." I retort.

He shrugs. "I got nothin' to tell ya, sweet cheeks. Why don't ya stop pretending, anyways?"

"Excuse me?"

"Ya obviously want a piece of old Bruiser. Coming across here pretending you're looking out for me... ha! It's okay, you just wanted to be close to me. I get it. Shall we take this back to yours?"

I roll my eyes and jump to my feet, and to my horror he copies me.

"Result!" He cries.

"Sit back down." I order, my cheeks flushed. "I'm done with you."

I'm aware of his eyes watching me as I cross the street and head towards home, and as much as I don't want to, I wonder how I look to him, and whether my bum looks big in the jeans I'm wearing. The fact that that thought even crosses my mind makes me furious with myself.

Wilson Bruiser is intolerable. A sexist pig. A thief!

But, for some reason, I'm not convinced that he's a murderer.

11

SAGE

*T*he three of us sit in an awkward silence until Connie bursts into the house, fury written all over her face.

"It went well, then?" I joke, but her look shoots me down and she goes straight to the kitchen and fills the kettle.

"I'll get a black coffee, please." Taylor says with a shy smile. Adele's transformed their home into a natural hell, banning caffeine and anything else that sounds like fun. Like the addict he is, he sniffs out his next hit of coffee whenever he can when he's not home.

Connie makes the two of them a drink without saying a word, and then joins us in the living room, where she cups her drink in her hands and folds her legs underneath her on the couch.

"So, Connie?" Taylor asks, glancing at his watch. He's on duty and we had to plead to get him to agree to come over, so my sister really needs to get with it and start talking. "You wanted this meeting? Do you have information?"

She lets out a deep sigh. "I spoke to Wilson Bruiser, and

I know he's a suspect and he should be, but I don't think it's him."

"Did you call me over here to tell me that?" Taylor asks, friendliness gone now he's got his coffee.

"No, of course not. I think we should be working together to solve this case and I wanted to make sure we're all on the same page." She says.

"Okay." Taylor says. "Let me do a little overview, then. Right now, our attentions are focused on Wilson Bruiser and Lovey Lovegoode. Both suspects because of the same motive - to get the journal."

"And the dagger belongs to Lovey." Sage says. "You've interviewed him about that?"

Taylor looks down at the carpet. "He's out of town."

"What?" Connie barks. "He's gone on the run!"

"No." Taylor says. "He's giving a talk in Arizona. It's been scheduled for months. Now, if he doesn't come back in two days' time like he should, then we'll start to wonder if he's ran away. At the moment, he's a man keeping a work commitment. Nothing suspicious there."

I groan.

"You're calling him in as soon as he gets back?" Patton asks.

"Let's talk about Wilson Bruiser." He says, dodging the question. "You guys think it could be him?"

"It's a possibility." Connie says.

"He's definitely a rule breaker." I say. "He turned up here the other day, completely uninvited."

"Oh, he's a total maverick, I don't doubt that. But plenty of people break rules and cause trouble without ever killing someone." Patton says.

"I don't think it's him." Connie says.

"You've already said." Taylor says, with a sigh. "But what's that based on? A feeling?"

"I guess so." Connie admits. "He just seems to not care that much, about anything. I can't imagine him being driven to violence over a diary."

"He has lost a hand, remember." I say. "So he clearly can be driven to violence."

"That wasn't through violence." Patton says, and we all turn and look at him. "I did some research. He had gangrene in his hand. It was amputated."

I let out a gasp. "Eww! Amputated? Are you serious?"

Patton nods. "It fits his wild image more to pretend it was from some battle, but the dude just got gangrene."

"That makes my belief that he isn't violent even stronger, then." Connie says.

"Maybe you're right." Taylor says. "I'll call him in for questioning too."

"What shall we do?" I ask.

"Keep your ears out. I think we're getting close. Try to find the journal, too." Taylor says, and slurps the dregs of his coffee and gets to his feet. "I'll be going. Good to catch up."

The door slams behind him and Patton takes a breath.

"I'm not happy about working a case with that man." He says.

"You've got to put your grudge with him to one side." Connie says, tone firm. "This is more important than you two not liking each other."

Patton shakes his head and I can feel the tension coming off him in waves.

"Come on." I suggest. "Let's go for a walk."

Mystic Springs is a hella pretty town, as the kids would say.

The streets are wide and tree-lined and the mountains that surround the town stand majestically in the background, as old as time itself, entirely uninterested in whatever human dramas are happening. They're a constant reminder of how short life is - as if I need one.

The only noises are the distant roar of the springs up ahead, the occasional chirrup of a bird, and the hum of a lawn mower. The sun is warm on my ghostly skin and the man I'm walking - *floating* - with is so close to me that I know, even though he isn't touching me, he wants to. I'm tempted to reach across and hold his hand but call me old-fashioned, that's for him to do.

And so we stroll closer to the springs in a comfortable silence, me focused on whether or not he's going to hold my hand, and Patton? Who knows? His mind is probably still back simmering about his rivalry with Taylor Morton.

The relative silence is broken by a shrill laugh, but there's nobody around. We're almost at the springs now, and I sit on the bench overlooking the water, waiting for Patton to join me. He doesn't. He walks up to the railings and looks out at the water, so I go to join him.

A movement to my left catches my attention.

"Oh, you naughty boy!" A voice calls. Lavinia Blackbottom the fourth stands at the edge of the railings, her back to the springs, a cell phone clutched to her ear. She's not facing me, but she doesn't have to. Her money coat makes her recognisable instantly.

Patton looks at me and raises an eyebrow. "I wonder who she's talking to."

"Mm-hmm, I bet you'd like that." She purrs into the phone. "It's been a long time since Bunny had new shoes."

I move closer so I can hear better. There's a large red baneberry plant between me and her and I position myself behind it. Given the bush and my ghostly appearance, not to mention how focused she is on her conversation, I doubt she'll see me.

"Oh, no, you shouldn't. You've already given me my allowance this month, sugar. I can struggle by with the ones I have." She says, voice so loud it's clear she has no idea anyone else is around. "Okay, love, go on then. Shall I walk over to you? Oh! You'll pick me up? You're adorable. I can't wait to see you!"

"We've heard enough." Patton hisses, and I don't agree, but Lavinia ends the call then without so much as a good-bye. She walks away from the springs, back towards town, without as much as a glance in our direction.

"Well, that's not very women's lib of her, is it?" I say with a laugh. "She's clearly got a sugar daddy paying her way."

Patton shrugs. "It's nothing to do with us."

"She's trotting her way around town pretending to be a leader for independent women, and she's got someone giving her an allowance." I say.

"You sound jealous." Patton teases.

"I am!" I admit with a laugh. "But, importantly, I've never pretended to be independent."

"Oh, I'd say you're a strong independent woman, Sage." He says, and I feel my stomach flip. "It's one reason why I haven't sent you flowers or anything else like that."

"Huh?"

"It can be a bit intimidating, you know, being around someone as strong and beautiful as you."

"Are you winding me up?" I ask, cautious.

He shakes his head, and I'm sure he's moving in. You know, moving in for the kiss. That moment every woman dreams of with a man she's attracted to. It's happening, it's happening, it's happening, and I'm so out of practice I can't remember whether I should close my eyes or keep them open, and the risk of course is that if I close my eyes and I'm wrong, I could be stood with my lips puckered and my eyes closed and look like a fool. In that scenario, what would a man do? Maybe he'd see the lips puckered, panic and run away? Or maybe he'd see them, pity me, and give me a reluctant kiss. I'm not sure which option is worse.

And before I know it, as he moves closer, I'm moving away. Just a fraction of an inch. You'd hardly notice, really, unless you were moving closer to me without getting any closer. I see the recognition in his eyes, the very moment when he understands - *she's moving away from me.*

And I have to do something, because I want this kiss. I want it so badly I daren't let it happen, but I don't want to stop him trying.

God himself appears to be shining down on me in that moment, because right when I need one, I have an epiphany.

"What about Lavinia?" I blurt out.

"Huh?" Patton says, as he moves back to standing upright and rubs his chin. "She's not really my type, Sage."

"No!" I cry. "Why isn't Lavinia a suspect?"

Patton looks at me for a moment and then cracks a smile. "Geeze, you never stop thinking about the case, do you? Come on, Sage, I thought we were relaxing for a while."

"Sorry." I say. "But don't you think it's worth looking into? I could be on to something, right?"

He shrugs. "I think it's Lovey. His house spooked me, you know? It's like a temple of historic objects."

"I know, but lots of people collect things without killing anyone over it." I say, hearing the whine in my voice. I hate it when I sound whiny, it's so unattractive. I shake my head and flash Patton a smile. "Anyway, it popped in my head and I wanted to mention it, but you know best, Sheriff."

He grins. He loves being called that, and I love knowing that he loves being called that.

If I have one skill in life (or the afterlife) it's finding a person's weak spot. And his, I know, is that in his heart he's still the true Sheriff of Mystic Springs.

He grins and reaches out his hand for mine, and we stare out at the springs in silence.

"So, she's got a rich person giving her an allowance?" Connie asks as she washes dishes in the kitchen. The room stinks. She made some kind of low-fat curried noodles for dinner and they looked as bad as they smelt. "Alright for some, isn't it."

I shrug. "Isn't it a bit two-faced for her to be all about women's independence when she's basically got a sugar daddy?"

Connie groans as she rinses the bubbles from her bowl and places it on the draining board. "Are you surprised?"

"Well..." I say, but the question stumps me. Am I surprised? Did I really expect better from a woman who leaves the house some days with a coat decorated with $50 notes, and nothing underneath? "Anyway, why are you eating this rubbish? That microwave meal, now these noodles?"

"Oh." Connie says, cheeks flushed. "I'm trying to watch what I eat."

"And only eat cardboard? Come on, Connie, this isn't real food."

Connie is an excellent cook. The time I visited her, with my daughters, back when I was alive and eating, her home-made dinners were pretty much the highlight of the trip for me. I had a lot on my mind back then, hippy person trapped in a small town that I was, but I'd turn up at her dining table for every meal convinced that she couldn't do better than the last meal she's prepared, and they just kept getting better.

A memory of her peach cobbler pops in my mind and I'm virtually drooling.

It's easy to see how she's become she size she is, and it's pretty darn sad to see her living on zero calorie ready meals.

"I just thought I should try and get more healthy." She says, scrubbing the pan furiously in the sink. "You should support me."

"I'll support you if you're eating apples, but this stuff isn't food. How can you even tolerate it after decades of eating your real food?"

She turns and flicks washing up bubbles at me, and I feel the dampness of them as they fly through me and on to her kitchen floor.

"Okay. I'll butt out." I say, hands raised. I wouldn't mind a water fight, but I know she'd get annoyed at some point, probably when she saw the state of the floor that would need cleaning. Connie's moments of rash madness are always followed quickly by the return of her practical head. "In other news, how do you think the meeting went earlier?"

"Hmm." Connie says as she lets the water out of the sink and dries her hands on a pink and white striped cloth that she's had for years. I can remember drying my own hands on it when I was visiting as a living person. "It's strange."

"Strange?"

"I don't really understand why Sheriff Morton is working with us." Connie says. "Especially as he doesn't seem to be doing much himself."

"Maybe that's the point. He knows his head isn't in the right place, so he gets us to work for free and then he'll take all the credit."

Connie frowns. "I don't want to believe that about him."

"Why? Because you're friends with his wife?"

She laughs but then purses her lips. "I don't think I am friends with his wife."

"You were out with her, getting drunk? Of course you are."

"Nah." Connie says with a shrug. "She lets me keep her company if I visit her, but I hear nothing from her when I sit and wait for her to get in touch. And, she wants to leave town."

"She just got here."

"I know. She's not happy here."

"Maybe that's why Taylor's distracted?" I suggest. "Pressure to leave?"

"Oh, I don't know. I don't want to talk about it." Connie says, and I see the fear in her eyes. Fear of rejection. Fear of loneliness. Fear of liking a friend more than they like her.

"Hey, that reminds me. Why hasn't Lavinia been considered as a suspect?"

Connie looks at me and purses her lips. "Good question."

"Right? It is, isn't it?" I say, trying not to gloat.

"How about we ask Sheriff Morton?" She says, and I groan.

"How about we just accept that the man isn't very good at his job, and get on with solving this case ourselves."

"With the one true Sheriff, who you just happen to have an eye for?" Connie teases.

"Fine." I say. "Let's ask him. But if he doesn't start doing some work soon, we need to forget him."

"Deal." She agrees, and then shakes her head at the damp spots on the kitchen floor.

See, I told you.

We visit Sheriff Morton at the station, figuring we can't drag him out to us every time we need to speak to him. A cop's leaving just as we arrive, and sloppily he lets us in without even asking who we are. Luckily, we're not the murderer and we just go up to the first floor and find Taylor sitting at his desk, staring out across the main street.

He doesn't hear us walk in, he's so engrossed in his thoughts, and Connie raps on the glass of his office door to blast him out of his thoughts.

"Oh, hey ladies." He says. A line of four empty coffee cups stands on his desk.

"Good job we're not Adele." I quip, eyeing the cups.

"Oh, she never comes down here." He says with a laugh. "I know I'm safe here."

"Hmm." I say, thinking back to him leading Lavinia through the building. Ain't that the truth. I wonder if Taylor could be her mystery benefactor, but can't imagine his small-town Sheriff's wage would be enough to support her lifestyle.

"We need to run something by you." Connie says. "About the case."

"Sure." He says.

"I think we should look at Lavinia Blackbottom as a suspect."

Taylor coughs, then reaches for the calendar that hangs on his wall. He inspects it and then places it on his desk. "She didn't do it."

"How do you know?" I ask, narrowing my eyes.

"She was here." He says, and points to the calendar. My eyes find the date of Emelza Shabley's murder, one of the few dates with any writing on at all.

"Fundraising meeting?" Connie reads aloud. The writing is in a distinctive purple ink.

He nods. "Lavinia's leading quite an ambitious campaign to get more funds coming into Mystic Springs. I was here all evening with her, discussing the plans."

"What kind of fundraiser?" I ask.

"I can't really say." He says, shifting in his seat a little as he returns the calendar to the wall. "It's early days."

"Oh." I say, the disappointment in my voice palpable.

"It was a good line of thinking, though, Sage. Well done." Taylor says, and if there's one thing I hate it's being patronised.

"Come on, we're done." I say, and I don't even wait for Connie, I float out of there.

She finds me in the parking lot, waiting for her.

"What got into you?" She asks, out of breath after her dash down the stairs and out to find me.

"He's so patronising." I whine. darn, whining again. What's happening to me?

"I don't think he was being patronising." Connie soothes. "He said it was a good idea, and it was. Let's just focus our energy on the suspects we've got, hey?"

"He's clearly not concentrating." I say.

"I know." Connie admits. "He must be really worried about baby Axel."

"I thought the kid was fine now?" I ask. Maternal instincts are not high in this one.

"He is, as far as I know." Connie says. "But Taylor was there in the car with him when he took ill. It might have traumatised him."

"I think a Sheriff needs to be able to handle some trauma." I say with a shrug. "Anyway, it's not my problem. Let him daydream all he wants. But I'm making sure we take the credit when we solve the case."

"Now you're talking!" Connie says with a grin.

"What do you know about Lovey Lovegoode?" I ask, because she's been on her computer constantly, learning all she can about Mystic Springs, and I can't imagine that the historian himself isn't all over the articles she's been reading.

"Well, he was married." She says.

"I'm not surprised." I say. She looks at me curiously. "The man's handsome! He just happens to be a weirdo."

"Sage!" She cries. "He isn't a weirdo! Plenty of people like antiques."

"Weirdos." I mutter under my breath. "Where's the ex-wife?"

"No idea." Connie says. "We won't struggle to find her, though, if she's kept her married name."

"Why, what's she called?"

"Lovell."

I stop floating and stare at my sister. "Lovell? Lovell Lovegoode?"

"Yep." She says, and she can't hold it in any longer, she bursts into laughter.

"Did he hand pick her for the name? He must have, surely?" I say, opening my eyes wide. If I didn't think the historian was a weirdo before, I definitely do now. Although his ex-wife is just as bad, for taking his name.

Lovey and Lovell Lovegoode.

Unbelievable.

12

CONNIE

*A*s I predicted, Lovell Lovegoode isn't hard to track down at all.

The apparent opposite of her former husband, she's active on every social media platform you can think of, and dozens you've never heard of. Her accounts are wide open, and Sage and I spend a pleasant evening reading her status updates and poring over her photos posted in the two years since her split with Lovey.

It appears that social media was a no-go during her married days, and she's more than making up for lost time.

A keen player of online games, she automatically updates her feed most hours to say that she needs a gaming friend to send her hay for her gaming farm, or to celebrate that her gaming hospital has successfully treated 10 patients in a row.

And splattered in around these game updates are her real updates, which you can recognise instantly because of the magical essays she crafts, full of heart emojis and exclamation marks.

She's beautiful, though. Her images show her to be

Amazonian with her deep brown skin and her everlasting legs. If I was going to have a girl crush, it would probably be on Lovell Lovegoode.

She's immediately responsive to my friend request and my private message, and eager to meet.

And so, before dawn, Sage and I set out into the mountains, along winding lanes and gravel paths until we reach her home, a beautiful cabin nestled in the treetops. Lovell won't be able to see Sage, as she lives outside of the town borders, but Sage insists on coming along. She'll sit quietly nearby so she can listen, she promises.

Lovell opens the door and it's clear instantly that she doesn't use any filters on the photos she posts. She's every inch the goddess she looks like on screen, and I self-consciously glance down at the muffin top riding over my linen pants.

"Good morning!" She calls out, and she's as American as apple pie, all white teeth, enthusiasm and daisy dukes. "I got some sweet tea for us, shall we sit out here? The view's so lovely as the sun comes up. Thanks for coming out so early!"

"Oh, thanks for having me." I say as she leads me to a deck at the side of the cabin, kitted out with a small table and two chairs. The sweet tea jug and two glasses are already out there, and I take a thirsty gulp when she pours my glass. She sits on the other chair, looks out over the view of the trees and the valley in the distance, and then turns her attention to me. "So. Lovey?"

"Yes, Lovey." I say with an awkward smile.

"Your hair is adorable, by the way." She says, and it's the most unexpected thing I could hear from this beauty. "I wish my hair would curl. It's so flat and lifeless."

"Are you kidding me?" I ask, looking at the sheen on her long, dark locks. Sure, her hair is poker straight, but I'd swap my flyaway frizz for straight hair any day. "Your hair's amazing."

"Oh, stop." She says, batting the compliment away. "You know, it's been two years since I saw or spoke to Lovey, so I don't know how much I can tell you."

"I'm sure anything you can share will be helpful. How did you two meet?"

"Online." She says with a reminiscing smile.

"Lovey was online?" I ask in surprise.

"Oh no, he hates the internet. No, he had a buddy who was teasing him, saying Lovey's name was so good, any wife he had would have to have a great name that would go with it. I was doing some modelling back then, so I was fairly well-known online. His friend remembered that he'd seen my name and said Lovey should marry me, and I guess Lovey liked the idea."

"That's wild." I say. Sure, the name might have sparked his interest, but her looks couldn't have hurt, either.

"The friend of his contacted me and arranged a blind date. It was all pretty mad. I have no idea why I said yes."

"And when you met?"

She lets out a dry, throaty laugh. "Oh, man, total nightmare. He was such a bore. Spent the entire dinner talking about antique cash registers."

"I'm guessing he won you over." I say with a smile.

"Well, I guess so too, but I look back and I don't know how. We had nothing in common. I'm such a regular girl, ya know, I love my modern comforts and he was living in the past. He managed to convince me to close all my online accounts, and that pretty much ended my modelling days. It was just a really silly time in my life."

"Wow." I say. "He was so against the internet that he didn't want you using it?"

She nods. "It's my own fault, ya know. I should have stood my ground. But he was older than me, and he seemed so wise. He treated me well, doted on me like a princess really. The marriage was fine as long as we didn't have to be together much. I'd find excuses to work away, because he wouldn't text or anything, so it was like a few days of bliss."

"Was he ever... did he ever hurt you?"

"Like, what, like hit me?" She asks, eyes wide. Her skin is so clear I could lick it. "Oh no, he never had any reason to. I was a pretty good girl. He said no internet, I got rid of the internet, ya know?"

"What made you leave?" I ask, taking another sip of my sweet tea.

"I had this friend, who'd got me lots of modelling jobs, and he rang me - I kept my cell phone, that's the one thing I wouldn't get rid of. He rang me and said there was this big job coming up over in Florida. And I went, and I earnt a lot of money, and I was gone for so long it just kind of seemed like the marriage was over, even though we hadn't spoke about it. Lovey hadn't made any contact with me while I was gone, and honestly I was having such a good time out there, it kinda felt like the whole marriage was something I'd imagined, ya know? I came back and stayed with a friend, found this place and moved in, and got my lawyers to serve the divorce papers on him."

"Wow." I say. "How did he react?"

"I can't say he was bothered." She says with a shrill laugh. "Maybe he thought I was as dull as I thought he was!"

"Do you know what happened over in Mystic Springs recently?" I ask.

She shakes her head. "I don't follow the news, it's all bad news. Is it Lovey? Is he okay? I feel bad now for sayin' all that, I don't wish the man bad or anything."

"Oh no, he's fine." I reassure her. "But someone was killed a few days ago. A woman named Emelza Shabley."

Lovell stares at me blankly.

"She claimed to have an old journal that revealed that Mystic Springs was founded by a man." I say.

A faint recognition flashes in her eyes. "Ohhhhh, it's meant to be a woman, right? I think I remember Lovey telling me about that. He went to some auction to bid on part of the original waggon that that woman had owned."

"He did?" I say, stunned. If Lovey's tried to own historic items relating to the founding of Mystic Springs before, that makes it even more obvious that he must have badly wanted the journal.

She nods and takes a sip of her sweet tea. "He came home in a furious mood that day. Some city slicker had bid way more than Lovey thought it was worth, so he'd stopped bidding, but he really wanted it."

"Did he have a strong interest in local history?"

Lovey shook her head. "No stronger than any other history, really. He was a man obsessed with the past. Hold on, do you think Lovey hurt that woman?"

"It's a possibility I'm looking into." I say with a regretful smile.

"Wow." She breathes.

"You probably know him better than anyone. Do you think he'd kill someone, to get his hands on an antique?"

She stares out at the trees for a few seconds, pondering the question. "When we were dating, we went out to a BBQ joint one night, and it was early days. I kept turning up for dates and I kept leaving wondering why I'd gone out with him again, but he was so sweet and he gave me lots of presents. I had on this antique necklace that Lovey had given me. He loved to see me wear it. And this particular night, some bums were in the bar making comments about me. It got pretty heated, they were intense, ya know? And Lovey was ignoring it all, until this one guy reached over and tried to touch the necklace. Well, Lovey was out of his seat like you wouldn't believe. He had the poor drunk on the floor and he was hitting him over and over again. And when they got split up, I was about to thank Lovey, ya know, for protecting me. But he looked at me and I'll never forget his words - *that necklace is rare, you nearly let him touch it!"*

"He wasn't protecting you at all." I murmur.

"He was protecting the thing that was valuable to him." She says with a faraway smile. "I should have seen the warning signs then. But, to answer your question, yes, I think Lovey could kill for an antique. He gets so obsessive. I could see him, not planning to hurt someone, but flying into a blind rage maybe. I can definitely see that."

"Does he have a police record?" I ask, wondering why Sheriff Morton hasn't picked up on it if so.

"Erm, I don't know." She says. "I stormed out of that place, I didn't wait around to see if the cops had been called. I was still doing shoots then, I couldn't have my name mixed up with that stuff."

"Of course." I say. "Are you modelling again now?"

She nods. "Luckily, I had enough contacts who were pleased to hear from me when I left. The job in Florida helped. I owe a lot to that one friend who offered me the Florida gig... it showed I could still do it, ya know. I'm flying this morning to do a shoot, that's why I had to ask you to come so early."

"It must be a glamorous life!" I gush and I suck in my belly a little as my eyes are drawn to the concave stomach hiding under Lovell's cami.

She shrugs. "It's a job."

"But you get to travel, and..."

"Travel is not glamorous." She says with a throaty chuckle. "Trust me, I'm not big enough for anyone to pay for me to fly first class, so it's hours flying coach, waiting around in airports, and then more hours of people fussing over my hair and make-up. It can be so bitchy too. Some of the girls are a nightmare. That's why I love it here, my little hideaway in the woods, where I can just grab my shorts and brush my hair and I'm ready."

I ignore the subtle suggestion that she's wearing no make-up, because the idea that this woman is that attractive naturally is more than I can handle as I sit there feeling my forehead dampen with sweat and knowing that my belly button has been swallowed up in between two rolls of stomach fat.

"Well, I should let you get going." I say. I catch Sage's eye. True to her word, she's been waiting around by the trees and hasn't made a sound.

"It was really nice to meet you." Lovell says, and she scoops me into a hug that is more bone than I'm used to. I pull away quickly, awkward that she will have felt my wobbles in just as surprising a way. "Can you tell me, what's going to happen to Lovey?"

"We're still investigating right now." I say. "Don't tell him I was here, please? It would threaten the case."

"Oh, don't worry, I haven't had any contact with him. I'm not going to change that. Good luck with it all. You know your way back out of here? Carry on up the hill and there's a turning spot, then come back on yourself. The roads get a bit challenging if you try to get out the other way."

"Thanks Lovell, it's been great to meet you." I say, and I walk back towards my car as she disappears into her little hideaway.

. . .

"She. Was. Beautiful." Sage exclaims as soon as we're back in the car. "Did you see her skin? It was flawless!"

"I know." I agree. "I can't help thinking a lifetime of those low fat meals won't get me looking as good as she does."

"Well, her body's her business." Sage says. "It'll be written in all her contracts, if she gains weight she'll be out."

I hadn't considered that. "She's clearly a nice person, too. There's more to her than her looks. It must be quite frustrating being judged on her appearance all the time."

"Hmm." Sage murmurs. "I'd happily give her life a whirl."

I smile to myself. Sage has always been desperate for adventure and freedom. I can imagine the novelty of being told what to wear and how to stand and where to look would wear off very quickly for her.

"And she thinks Lovey's capable of murder."

"I'd be very interested to see if he has a police record." I say as I turn on the small piece of gravel path. There's just enough space for a car to maneuver without reversing off the path and into the grassy slope. I say a silent prayer as I do the final turn and manage to straighten up facing back down the winding path. "Geeze, I wouldn't fancy this drive every day."

Sage grins at me. "Lovell's desperate to show she's not just a glamour puss, hey, living out here like a red neck."

"Sage!" I scold. "I like her. You think she's reliable?"

My sister shrugs and I sense her distraction.

"I'm sorry, is this murder investigation taking too much of your time?" I ask.

"Patton invited me to breakfast." She says, with a shy smile.

"What a waste of time. You can't eat or drink." I say.

"It doesn't matter!" Sage objects. "It's the experience of it, the smell of coffee and banana muffins. I think it's a cute idea."

"Well, is it a date?" I ask, slipping too easily into the interested friend role. I've been playing it my whole life, and just once I'd like to be the one with an exciting date coming up, not the one hearing about someone else's.

"I think so." She admits, and in her tone I hear the girlish excitement she's had throughout her whole life every time a boy - or a man - has shown an interest in her. I grin, because her happiness is contagious. She loves the highs and even the lows of this cycle. It's like a drug to her. She loves it the way I love carbs.

"We'd better get you home, then." I say, and as we finally get off the rickety gravel paths on to the main road, I accelerate and let out a whoop.

"What's got into you?" Sage asks, sceptical.

"I just like seeing you happy." I say, and I drive into Mystic Springs, past the high school where the caretaker is collecting garbage, past the pizza joint that's buzzing each afternoon but closed now, and past our house. I screech to a stop outside Screamin' Beans, catching the attention of Ellie Bean who is setting a menu on each of the outside tables. She glances up from her work and gives a wave.

"I'm early." Sage says in horror.

"You're welcome." I tease.

"No, I mean, I can't be here first." She hisses, slumping down low in the passenger seat. I shake my head and undo my seat belt.

"I'm going to grab a coffee. You can hide out here or come in with me." I say, opening the driver door.

Sage groans. "Fine. Let's pretend we're having a meeting before I fit him in for breakfast, that sounds impressive, doesn't it?"

"Very impressive." I soothe. The cool of the A/C hits me as I walk into the coffee house. A country song plays out, all tractors and heartbreak, and Godiva snores from the most comfortable seat in the house.

Ellie makes her way back to the counter and washes her hands.

"Morning, ladies." She says, tucking a strand of auburn hair behind her ears. "Cappuccino?"

"Please, Ellie." I say. "How are things? Are you hearing much about the Emelza Shabley murder?"

She shakes her head. "It's old news, it seems. People don't seem to have any faith that it's going to get solved."

"What? Why would they think that?"

She glances towards the corner of the coffee house, where Sheriff Mortion sits nursing a large mug. "He's spending a lot of time here. A lot of time clearly not working. It's not reassuring seeing the Sheriff drink coffee while there's a murderer on the loose."

"What's wrong with him?" I wonder aloud.

Sage huffs behind me. "The man is a liability. Patton warned you. It's the wife I feel for."

"Oh, I wouldn't worry about her." Ellie says. "Word on the street is she won't be around much longer."

"What?" I ask. I knew she wasn't happy here but I thought we were friends. If she's planning leaving, I thought she would have told me before it became general gossip.

Ellie shrugs. "Oh, you'd have to ask him. Looks like he's got nothing better to do!"

"I might just do that." I say quietly, and I gaze across the coffee house to Sheriff Morton. A man with the weight of the world on his shoulders, clearly, as he stares down into his mug. His mind is focused somewhere, but it clearly isn't on finding out who killed Emelza Shabley.

13

SAGE

*W*e're stationed outside Lovey Lovegoode's house, across the street, on one of the dozen benches dotted around town in memory of Atticus Hornblower. Rumour has it that he funded the benches himself, with money tucked away in some secret account that couldn't ever be formally connected to him. The bronze plaque declares him to be a *great leader and lover of Mystic Springs.*

It's unfortunate wording, because trust me, I don't want to imagine Atticus as a lover in any sense of the word.

"He's late." Patton says, arms crossed, stifling a yawn.

We convinced Connie to ring his hotel and a dopey receptionist told us the time he'd checked out without a second thought for his confidentiality. The drive back should take three hours, so we allowed him four. The man might need a toilet break, ya know.

"Has it been four hours exactly?" I ask.

"A little over."

"Maybe he grabbed lunch." I say. "Or hit traffic."

"Maybe." Patton says, but neither of us are convinced.

Lovey Lovegoode is probably long gone, driving in the opposite direction, never to be seen again. That's what I'd do if I were guilty. Not that I've spent a huge amount of time planning what I'd do if I killed someone, but surely putting as much distance between yourself and the crime is Killing 101?

"The police will track his car, surely." I say.

"Oh, yeah, all that can be done." Patton says. "If he's smart, he'll ditch the car. He's got time since we're the only ones looking for him."

I sigh.

"Talk of the devil." Patton says, and we both look down the road as an old Corvette appears in view. Bright red, roof down, and inside it, Lovey Lovegoode returns.

He turns the vehicle onto his drive, slows to a stop, and a good ten minutes pass without him opening the door.

"Think he's considering making a run for it?" I ask.

"Nah." Patton says. "He wouldn't drive all the way back and get spooked because we're sitting on a bench. Let's just go and talk to him."

We find him rifling through the car, filling a plastic bag with rubbish. He's a travel eater. Such a beautiful classic car and it's piled high with empty coffee cups, bags of sweets, and the sugar from the sweets. The passenger seat has a chocolate stain where one of his goodies has melted.

Patton clears his throat and makes Lovey jump.

"Can I help?"

"We need to talk to you, can we go inside?" Patton says. He flashes his Sheriff's badge, which actually gives him no authority since he went and died, but impresses a fair number of people, who agree to talk to him and open up as if he's still law enforcement.

Maybe it's like being the President. Once a POTUS, always a POTUS.

"Sure thing." Lovey says. "Give me a minute."

He returns to filling the plastic bag with his junk, and then climbs out of the car, leading us up onto his small veranda and inside the house. I try to look surprised at the interior, as if I've never set foot in the house before. Well, I haven't set foot inside, since I don't have feet any more.

"You erm, don't want a drink?"

"No, no, we can't drink. But thanks." Patton says.

Lovey leads us into the room that houses most of his collections, and stands, hands in pockets, waiting for us to talk.

"We're working with Sheriff Morton on the Emelza Shabley murder case." Patton says. "We have some questions for you."

"Don't ya normally call people into the station to be questioned?"

"We thought this would be more discrete."

Lovey nods. "Well, how can I help?"

"Can we all sit down?" Patton asks.

"Sure." Lovey says, and pulls out a chair. We sit across from him, as if it's a police interrogation, which I guess it is. My hands are shaking with nerves and adrenaline.

"I need to start by asking what you know about the murder?"

"As much as anyone else, I guess." He says with a shrug. "I heard about it. Awful."

"Did you know her?"

"Not really." He says. "I keep myself to myself, really. And I travel a lot. I've just got back from a few days away."

"What exactly do you do?" I ask. "I mean, history is clearly your thing, but..."

He cracks a huge grin, happy to get on to this topic. "I'm a historian. I buy antiques. I should sell them, but very often I find it hard to part with them. I mean, I do sell some things. Your friend, Sheriff Morton, I sold his wife a few things to furnish their new home. I also give lectures across the country, sometimes internationally, and I've had the occasional appearance on TV as a history expert. I've just been approached actually, thanks to Lavinia, to work as an advisor behind the scenes on a documentary series, I don't know if the details for that will work out, but it's fun to be considered."

"I bet." I say, but I can't imagine anything more dull. Spending all day checking that really old, fusty things are the right kind of old and fusty. Ugh.

"Where were you the night Emelza was killed?" Patton asks.

Lovey bristles. "Am I a suspect?"

"At the moment, you're helping with enquiries. If you're not willing to do that, we can make this more formal and go to the station."

"No, no." Lovey says. With a TV deal pending, he doesn't want word getting out that he's been taken in for questioning. "I can't remember where I was."

"You can't remember?"

"I could consult my day planner, but I only record my appointments. If I was at home, it will be empty."

"Would it help jog your memory if we said that you'd been in Screamin' Beans that day, where you were seen speaking to Emelza Shabley and arranging to visit her that evening to take a look at the journal she'd found?" I say.

"Ah, yes, yes, that would help, thank you." He says, pushing his glasses up his nose. "In that case, I was at home, alone, all night."

"But you said you'd visit Emelza."

"She didn't seem keen. I didn't go. I don't even know where she lives. Lived."

Patton clasps his hands together, holds eye contact with Lovey, and waits. It's a tactic he's told me about. How sometimes, all you need to do to get a suspect to trip themselves up is be quiet. Apparently people would rather confess to murder than handle an awkward silence.

Not Lovey, though. He breaks eye contact pretty quick and looks down at his hands, but he doesn't speak.

"Are you saying, on record, that you didn't visit Emelza Shabley's home at all on the night she was killed?" Patton says, his words clear and definite. There can be no misunderstanding him. He needs that to be obvious.

"Yes, sir." Lovey says.

"Do you know how she was killed?" Patton asks.

Lovey's cheeks flush. "I believe she was stabbed."

"You know that how?"

"I like to keep up with the news. I read the newspaper. I hear, erm, gossip."

"Do you own any knives? Daggers? Swords?" Patton asks.

"Well, of course." Lovey says. "I mean, I own a few. It's not really my thing, but if one comes up, I'll consider it. I don't tend to hang on to them, though, I'm happy to sell them on."

"Can we see the ones you have?" I ask.

"Sure." Lovey says with a shrug of his broad shoulders. "Follow me."

He leads us into the bathroom and opens the cabinet. Inside, one shelf has a small pile of items secured in bubblewrap.

"Oh." He says as he pulls the items out.

"What?"

"This is odd." He says, peering back into the small cabinet. "There should be... there should be four."

He walks back into the room and places the items on the table, where he opens each. "This is a Prussian hunting cutlass. Amazing condition. The handle's deer horn. Had a gentleman from Germany interested in this, would you believe? And then this, its a piper's dirk. Scottish, World War One. This one..." He says, handling the last. "is a Piha Kahetta, from Sri Lanka. Isn't it beautiful?"

"But there's one missing?" Patton says, trying to keep Lovey focused from wandering off on a tangent about ancient daggers. To say they're not his thing, his eyes have still glazed over as he talks about them. Please God, I hope I never have to talk to him about cash registers, his one true love.

"Yes, absolutely."

"What's it like?"

"Oh, stunning." Lovey says.

"Describe it."

"It's a Hungarian Air Force parade dagger, dates back to World War Two if not earlier. Not terribly valuable, I bought it with the Piha Kahetta, that's the one I really wanted. Old guy wouldn't split them up. I don't think he wanted the hassle of more viewers. So I took them both. He could see I was mad about the Piha Kahetta! They're the royal knives, you know. No way was I leaving without it."

"When did you last see it?"

"The Piha Kahetta? This is the -" Lovey says, stroking the straight-backed blade. It looks like the kind of thing I'd toss in the trash if I came across it. I've never had an eye for antiques, though.

"No. The dagger that's missing. When did you last see that?"

"I've got no idea." Lovey admits.

"Well, try. This is important."

"I honestly don't know. I live alone, I don't have many visitors, I've got no need to check that all of my things are where they should be."

"Why are they in the bathroom cabinet?" I ask.

He shrugs. "I've always put them there. I grew up in a gun house. My father schooled me on making sure anything dangerous wasn't kept out on show."

"Did he put his guns in the bathroom?" I quip.

"In a trunk in the basement." Lovey says. "I don't have a basement."

"Lovey, I need you to realise how serious this is. The dagger used to kill Emelza Shabley, it's been tested, it's yours."

Lovey drops the dagger that's in his hand and sinks down onto a seat at the table. "My goodness, it can't be."

"It is. We traced it back to the seller."

"Oh my." Lovey says. He clasps his head in his hands and begins to cry. "Can I make a call?"

"Who to?"

"I think I may need a lawyer."

"Do you want to make a confession?" I ask.

He sucks in a huge gulp and shakes his head. "I have nothing to confess, but I know my rights. I need a lawyer. Can I call one?"

"Do you have one?" I ask.

He looks at me aghast. "Why on Earth would I have one? I've never needed one before. I need to make some calls. I need to think. Can you leave now?"

"No." I scoff. "We need to get to the bottom of why your dagger was used to kill a woman you promised you'd be visiting that evening!"

"I can't explain that."

"Let's talk about the journal." Patton says. "You wanted it, didn't you?"

"Well, of course I did. I'm a historian, I want lots of things. I don't get them all."

"But you really wanted this? Like you said about that knife - you wouldn't let it go."

"The Piha Kahetta is different. Sentimental, really. I learnt about them in school."

"Where did you go to school?"

"Right here." He says, chest high. "Born and raised right in Mystic Springs."

"So surely a journal written about the founding of your town would be sentimental too?" I ask, and I see Patton glance at me and feel myself swell with pride too.

Lovey realises the trap he's walked in to, but too late. His eyes dart around the room, but no help can be found. "I'd never hurt anyone."

"Would Lovell agree with you about that?" I ask.

His cheeks turn flame red. Incensed, his mouth tightens. "How dare you? Have you spoken to her? You can't believe a word that woman says! She left me high and dry to go off with some model, did she tell you that? Did she tell you anything apart from how awful I am?"

"She told me lots of interesting things." I say.

"I need a lawyer." He says, and stands from the chair. We let him go, and hear him pacing in the hallway, then lifting the receiver of the phone and punching digits. "God darn it!"

"Are you ok, Lovey?" Patton asks, following him out into the hall. I remain in the room and look around, wondering where Lovey could have hidden the journal. If the man keeps daggers in his bathroom cabinet, there's no way to guess where he might be hiding the journal.

I look around anyway, but the place is creeping me out. There's something unnatural about being surrounded by so many old things. I've been twenty years dead and I've got a better grip on modern life than Lovey Lovegoode has.

"They're not answering." Lovey curses as he returns to the room. "Look, I know this doesn't look good. I do see that. But you have to let me speak to a lawyer, and then maybe I can come to the station and we can get this all cleared up? I'll help you in any way I can. I don't want this to get out, though, please. My reputation would be ruined."

"I don't know." I say. "Historian kills for historic item... it could launch your media career."

"I've got no interest in a media career. It's a necessary evil to spread the word, to bring me bookings for lectures. Please, have some respect. I've worked so hard for my career."

"And the journal would put you right at the top of your game." Patton says. "Your motive's clear. Your opportunity was right there. We know how you did it."

"You should just confess, it'll make things easier for you in the long run." I suggest.

"I've got nothing to confess to!" He cries, slamming his hand on the table so hard I instinctively jump back, even though he can't hurt me. As a spirit, I can't feel physical pain, and I've already died, but that instinct to move away from danger is hardwired into us all, I guess.

"Enough." Patton says, pushing himself in between me and Lovey.

Lovey trembles, his eyes wild. He says nothing but he knows. The mask has slipped. He's revealed his temper. His shadow side.

"Let's go." I say.

"Lovey, don't leave the town, okay? We'll talk to Sheriff Morton and then we'll be back. We can keep doing this the discrete way or we can haul you in so everyone sees. So don't make us have to hunt for you."

"And don't try to contact Lovell." I add, suddenly regretful for mentioning her name. The thought of her all alone in the woods makes a chill run down my spine.

"I've got no interest in contacting that woman." He says, and he collapses into the chair, his energy and power gone, like a huge bear defeated. "I can't believe this is happening."

"Well, I bet Emelza Shabley thought similar when you turned up at her house with a dagger." Patton says.

"Her house? Well, that proves it, I wasn't there! She lives in a waggon!" Lovey shouts, then realises what he has just admitted.

"Ah, so you do know where she lives." Patton says, casting a wink in my direction.

"This isn't fair." Lovey moans, but we're already heading down his hallway, and then out into the stifling warm air. The roads are empty, but the smell of a nearby barbecue floats over the lawns, and a small girl lies on her back on a nearby lawn, gazing up at the clouds.

"Did you used to do that?" I ask as we walk away, leaving a pitiful Lovey Lovegoode to await our next move.

"Look at the clouds? Nah. I was an all-action hero, too busy splashing in streams and building dens. I had the best den in the whole state. Kids used it for years after I'd grown up. Still think that's one of my best achievements in life." Patton says with a lazy smile. "So, what do you make of Lovey?"

"He's so screwed." I say. "We need Morton to get over there and arrest him ASAP."

"The things that drive people to kill will never stop amazing me. All this over a tattered old journal."

"A tattered old journal we still need to find." I say.

"We should search Emelza's waggon. I wonder if Lovey hid it there, knowing we'd suspect him and search his place."

"Ooh, that's a good idea."

"And then, I'd like to take you out for breakfast." Patton says, his voice clipped, nerves screaming out. "I mean, if you'd let me."

I flash him my most winning smile, the one that makes my eyes twinkle. "I'd love to."

14

CONNIE

I've purposely not contacted Adele, but the radio silence from her worries me.

What if baby Axel has taken a turn for the worse, and she'd desperately like some support but can't find the time to ask for it?

I'm not the kind of friend to risk leaving her like that, in need of help.

And so, I trudge down the road towards her home, enjoying that the evening has finally grown cooler. It's been a sweaty, sticky kind of day and I'm not thin enough for that heat. I can feel every single one of the extra pounds I carry on days like today, and the humidity is hell for my hair.

I groan as I walk up the path, already anticipating the whirr of Adele's AC unit and the reassuring tick of her ceiling fans. To say she hasn't been here long, she's made the house a beautiful home. I guess that's what an overachiever does when she's got no career to focus on, unlike me, who just apparently gets grumpy.

"It's not happening!" Taylor's scream stops me in my tracks just as I'm about to knock on the front door. I glance towards the living room window and see the shape of him by the glass. There's no way I can retreat back down the path without him seeing me and realising I've heard. I'll have to wait it out, right here.

"We're not staying." Adele replies, and her voice is the ice of the lawyer I've heard in her before. She's so in control, it stuns me a little. I grew up with a mum making it alone, no man around, but she was breaking her back to barely get by. And being single was hardly her choice. In the world I come from, a woman finds a man and tries her best to hold onto him, no matter how bad for her he might be. Adele is so strong, so independent, if she wants to leave, she'll up and go.

"You need to give this time." Taylor pleads. "This was such a quiet town. It's bad timing, that's all."

Adele scoffs. "No. I'm done talking about this. I can't believe you're arguing with me about it! There's a murderer on the loose! We all need to pack up and go."

"I can't just walk out halfway through a case…"

"We'll go ahead of you, then. Like we came here before you." Adele says.

"No, Adele." Taylor says, his own voice growing more firm. "They're my babies too. You're not allowed to take them across state, remember."

I bristle at this, the threat in his words.

"Don't you dare." She retorts.

"You signed it."

"You demanded it." She hisses.

"I know what you're capable of." He says, and I want to duck for cover from him then, at the audacity of his words.

"And I know what you're capable of, Taylor, let's remember why we ended up in this dump."

"You need to let that go." He says, tone soft again. He's

pushed it too far, he's the one who needs this to work out, to be smoothed over. This power balance within couples fascinates me. The way that, right down at the heart of it, there will be one of you who needs the other more. One who is more invested. One who will walk away, and one who will beg you to stay. And it's surprisingly difficult to predict which way it might go ahead of time. But here, as I listen to this awful argument, I have no doubt. It will be Taylor watching Adele leave.

As I think that, the energy in the room transforms, and I hear Adele's soft sobs. I glance across at the window and see her go to him and collapse into his arms.

"Don't threaten to take my babies away from me." He says as he wraps his arms around her.

I watch her body convulse and think, maybe I'm wrong. Maybe she talks a good talk. That's what lawyers do, right? They know how to say the right thing, how to craft a convincing argument. But would she really leave him? Would she take on life as a single mom of baby twins?

Who knows?

And why does it matter?

Because it's clear, as I stand watching the two of them, as I watch her hungrily reach for the buttons on his shirt and hear him moan, that they've forgotten this argument as quick as it started.

I force myself to look away, and take my chances walking down the path, leaving them to kiss and make up.

"Connie!" Finian Archbold calls to me from his Bentley GT, idling to a stop. I walk across to him, still feeling flushed from the scene at Adele's.

"Finian, how are you?"

"Excellent, my dear. You really must visit the castle again!"

"Oh, yes." I say, confused by the unexpected invitation.

I note the expensive looking shopping bags draped on the passenger seat, and he follows my gaze.

"Retail therapy?" I ask with a smile, wondering how it must feel to have endless wealth. Would shopping ever grow tiresome? Surely, the appeal of buying things is only there because there's a limit to what you can buy? Without that limit... to know that you could literally buy anything you fancied on any day, surely that would kill the fun?

"Not for me." He says quickly. "I'm not a shopper really."

"Oh." I say. "Well, it doesn't look like it!"

"They're for Lavinia." He says, then leans across and drops his voice. "She's finding it awfully hard since Emelza Shabley's death, you know. It goes against everything she believes in, a poor woman being killed like that."

"Quite." I say, wondering which version of Lavinia he knows, because it certainly isn't a version I've ever met.

"A few bits to cheer her up." He says with a grin, and I notice that one of the bags is from a lingerie shop. Everyone, it seems, has more of a romantic life than I do, even the so-called singles.

"That's very good of you." I say, and then I decide to just come out with it. What's the worst that can happen? If I'm wrong, he'll be flattered. "Don't you already do enough? With the allowance?"

"Ahh." He says, and his posture straightens as his chest inflates. "Well, yes. You could say that. But I'm able to do more, so why not?"

"Why not." I repeat, thinking I'd like someone to do enough for me, never mind the more on top.

"You must come back over." He urges. "Bring your sister. My Tobias would adore her."

"She really doesn't need any more men to adore her." I snap.

"Ahh... flighty is she?" He asks with a chuckle.

"No, she isn't. She's married, actually." I say, and immediately regret it. She's only been married on paper ever since she died and she won't appreciate me telling people about it. "Well, when she was alive, she was... erm..."

"Oh, Tobias too." Finian says. "Great chance to ditch the deadwood, so to speak, isn't it?"

I give a nervous laugh and look at my watch.

"I'm keeping you. I should have known. Forgive me." Finian says with an apologetic smile. "Just thought I'd say hello!"

I smile at him as he roars the engine, gives a little wave, and drives away.

I have no idea why I looked at my watch. I've got no plans and nobody waiting for my return.

An evening with the TV on, perhaps, watching young and beautiful people with no talent somehow captivate the country because they are young and beautiful. Or maybe I'll read instead, although my attention span for books has disappeared lately.

I know something's really wrong when I can't muster up the enthusiasm to dive into a new book.

*I*t's not a date, okay?

And I'd rather not talk about it.

Except to say this - I'm sitting, twirling my hair like every good girl learns in Flirting 101, and Patton Davey is giving more attention to that incompetent Sheriff than he is to me.

And, I'll say this. He totally made out like it was a date. He was all, *are you free? Would you like to have breakfast with me?* I know how people get invited to meetings, because trust me, Atticus Hornblower has given me way too many of those invitations over the years. And I try to say no whenever I can.

So I'm a pretty skilled meeting-dodger.

This was a date.

And I'm pretty darn annoyed that Patton has taken one look at Sheriff Morton, tucked in the corner of Screamin' Beans nursing a strong coffee and a packet of painkillers, and decided there's no time to waste, we need to discuss the murder.

There's nothing to discuss, as far as I can see. Lovey

Lovegoode did it and he needs arresting. Which only Sheriff Morton can do.

"Something's not adding up." Patton says through clenched teeth. "I've never seen a Sheriff so uninterested in solving a case."

"You said it yourself, he's not a very good Sheriff. And he's a cheat!"

"Well, sure, but he's not even pretending to investigate." Patton says. "My gut's telling me something's wrong."

"Your gut's probably just having ghost-pangs." I say, because I know mine is. This is the down side of coming out for breakfast. My stomach has convinced itself that it's hungry, even though I can't eat and haven't for two decades. Put it in front of this much bacon and the ghost-pangs are so believable I'm almost tempted to order something. I'm sure Connie would pick up the tab.

"I'm going to speak to him." Patton says.

"Oh, you're kidding me." I groan.

"Coming?" He asks, and he's in complete work mode now, there's no way of turning this back into a date.

"Fine." I whine. Whining again! This is not good.

Sheriff Morton doesn't even look up as we approach, and as we get so close that he feels our presence, he simply holds out his empty mug as if we must be staff.

"Erm..." Patton says, and clears his throat.

Sheriff Morton looks up and I see the disappointment on his face. "Can I help?"

"We need to talk." Patton says. "Shall we do it here, or?"

"Let's go to the station. Give me twenty minutes?" Sheriff Morton says, and he gets to his feet, leaving his empty mug on the table.

.   .   .

Eighteen minutes later, because if Patton believes one thing it's that you're late if you're on time, we find the police station in darkness and the parking lot empty.

"He's done a runner." Patton says.

"Why would he do that? He probably just had to run an errand. Maybe when he said twenty minutes, he meant twenty." I say, arms folded.

"Nah." He says as an old pick up truck drives down the main street, a heavy guitar beat booming out of the window.

"Maybe a call came in, an emergency." I suggest. I can't imagine that the Sheriff would disappear rather than speak to us, and I try not to look too smug when Sheriff Morton drives into the parking lot a moment later. "Ah, here he is."

"I've not got long." Sheriff Morton says as he unlocks the front door and leads us up into his office. As normal, his desk is a hot mess, and the line-up of empty coffee cups has doubled in number.

"You really need to hire a cleaner." I quip.

"It's not at the top of my priority list." He says, sitting with his hands in his lap. "What do you guys want?"

"We need some answers, Taylor." Patton says, using the Sheriff's name unusually.

Sheriff Morton blinks at us and begins to scratch behind his ear.

"We know who did it." Patton says.

"You do?" Sheriff Morton asks, leaning back in his chair.

"Lovey Lovegoode." Patton announces. "He has clear motive. He was seen wiping his prints from the waggon. The dagger's his. We've spoken to his ex-wife and know he has a history of violence, he might even have a police record. And we've spoken to him. He's got no alibi. You need to arrest him."

"Right..." Sheriff Morton says, slowly. "Sage, you think it's him too?"

"Absolutely." I say.

Sheriff Morton sighs.

"I need you to tell me something." Patton says. "Is there something happening here, something I should know about that means you can't work this case?"

Sheriff Morton blanches. "Like what?"

"Like an outside distraction?" Patton says, his meaning clear.

Sheriff Morton laughs. "God, no. Look, I've made my mistakes, but those days are behind me. I'll sort this out. Leave it with me."

"I"m not prepared to do that." I say, and my tone stuns both of the men nearly as much as it surprises me. "I've been dragged across here too many times to try and get you to do your job. Lovey Lovegoode needs to be arrested today, before anyone else gets hurt."

"You were incredible." Patton says, floating after me like an eager puppy dog. Sure, now he's interested.

"Well, it needed saying." I declare as I head back towards home. Connie should be in, and I want to sit down with her and forget about men and the murder case.

"I know it's past breakfast now, but how about lunch?" Patton suggests.

"Not now." I say. "I want some time on my own."

"Oh." He says, and his disappointment pushes up against my determination. He's a good man. I shouldn't be sulking because he still takes his responsibility as a Sheriff more seriously than Taylor Morton does.

"Look, I -" I begin, but he shakes his head.

"It's fine, Sage. There'll be another time." He says, forcing a smile. "I'll probably go back to Screamin' Beans, see what else I can hear. If you change your mind, come across? Bring Connie?"

"I'll see." I agree. He floats away and I watch him for a few moments as I stand by the front gate. I must be insane, turning away such a decent man. He continues down the street towards the coffee house, and I watch until he's out of sight.

It's like Connie's hosting a party and forgot to tell me.

The noise hits me first, a raucous din of people talking over each other. I'm tempted to slink away to the attic where I can get some peace and quiet, but curiosity wins and I walk through the house, following the noise.

In the lounge, Connie meets my eyes as soon as I appear in the doorway. Clearly, she's as happy to be hosting this get together as I am to walk back in and interrupt it.

Mariam Hornblower sits on the couch, her face a dozen different shades of red, as her father Atticus floats in front of her, in the middle of a lecture.

"Dad, please!" Mariam interrupts.

Next to her sits Desiree, Mariam's partner and boss, and next to her is her son Troy, who looks as delighted to be part of this conversation as any teenage boy would be.

"I'm just saying you're rushing in to it all!" Atticus bellows.

"Rushing in to what?" I ask.

"Living together." Connie says, with an eye roll.

"Erm, I think Mariam's old enough to decide for herself if she's ready." I say. Atticus can be insufferable sometimes.

Even his death hasn't stopped him suffocating his poor daughter.

"Thank you, Sage." Mariam says from the couch.

"Mom, can I go?" Troy asks.

Desiree nods. "We'll both go. Mariam, call me later?"

Mariam gives Desiree a smile but they make no attempt to say farewell to each other under Atticus' watchful eyes.

"I'll see you out." I offer, and I walk them out to the veranda. "What's brought all this on? And why's Connie been dragged into it?"

"God knows." Desiree says with a shake of her head. "I think Atticus thought Connie might take his side, or at least referee the conversation."

"Do you think it's because you're -" I begin, not knowing how to end the sentence without causing offence.

"Lesbians? Nah. Nobody's good enough for his daughter. Gender really isn't part of it. Come on Troy, let's get out of here. I've got a stack of marking to do and I know you have homework to finish."

Troy groans, perhaps regretting his eagerness to escape.

I wave as they walk away, and then listen to my first instinct and sneak away up to the attic, where the heat is stifling but the quiet is delicious. I take a seat on the old leather chair and close my eyes, welcoming the dreams that come.

Dreams of Lovey Lovegoode being arrested and convicted of murder come to me quickly, and then there's a whole-town celebration in which I'm brought up on stage and thanked for my detective work. There are talks of a life-size statue of me being erected in front of the police station, and I try to act demure while also making it clear that's an amazing idea.

Patton comes to me at the grand unveiling of the statue,

which manages to be incredibly beautiful but not quite as beautiful as me, so that people can say for centuries to come, *can you believe the real Sage Shaw was even more beautiful than this*? Patton goes down on one knee and proposes, promising to give me the happiest afterlife any spook has ever had, and it's a dream, so it doesn't matter that I'm already married. I say yes, and pucker up for the kiss I've been waiting for...

When I wake up, it's grown dark and the house is perfectly quiet. The air is cooler, so I guess it must be evening time. I've slept for hours.

I find Connie on the veranda, rocking in the chair.

"Hey, sleepy head." She greets me.

"Ugh." I moan. "Why did you let me sleep for so long? I needed to be alert today."

"How come?"

"I gave Sheriff Morton an ultimatum."

Connie looks at me wide-eyed.

"Oh, yeah." I say, enjoying having her hang on my every word. "I told him he had to arrest Lovey Lovegoode today."

"Or what?" She asks.

"What do you mean, or what?"

"You said you gave him an ultimatum?"

"Uh huh."

"Well, an ultimatum is, you do this or I will do that."

"Oh." I say, distant memories of high school English class returning to me. "Okay, I gave him an order then."

"Hmm." Connie says, and she glances at the horrid man's watch she insists on wearing on her chubby wrists. "I don't think he listened."

"What?" I ask. "I was very clear with him!"

"I'm sure you were. But it's after 8 and I saw Lovey not long ago."

"You're not serious." I say. I was sure I'd left Sheriff Morton under no doubt that I meant what I said. Maybe I should have given him an ultimatum. "What was he doing?"

"Going for a walk." Connie says. "Looked like he doesn't have a care in the world."

"Clearly he knows how rubbish our Sheriff is!" I exclaim. "Get ready, we're going to go and see Patton. This has gone too far."

"It doesn't make sense." Patton agrees as we sit with him in a corner of Screamin' Beans and take in the scent of Connie's cocoa. "We literally hand him the murderer on a plate, and he does nothing."

"He's useless." I moan. "Can't we just arrest him ourselves?"

"Ya know." Patton says, ignoring me. "I wonder if he disagrees with our theory and just doesn't want to upset us?"

"That doesn't sound like Sheriff Morton. I thought he'd like the chance to pull you down a peg or two." Connie says.

It's live music night at the coffee house and a petite woman with dyed grey hair (what's that all about?!) is setting up a microphone, a guitar strung over her shoulder. A group of college kids crowd around her but she moves as if she's unaware of them, so engrossed is she in preparing for her music.

"He's not like he used to be." Patton says. "He was this big character. In your face, way too confident, just a really arrogant mess. Now it's like he's got nothing left in him, no energy or fight or anything. He's just going through the motions."

"Well, he's too far off retirement to be slowing down. He's got a job to do and I don't see him with any other suspects." I say.

"As if he could find any suspects amongst the hovel he works in." Connie quips.

"Hmm." I say, the spark of an idea forming itself just out of my reach.

"What?" She asks.

"Nothing." I say, because how can you explain to a person that you think you're about to have an idea?

"Are you okay?" She asks as the girl taps the microphone and idly strums her guitar.

"I just... what was he doing with Lavinia that night?" I ask. "It makes no sense hat he'd be having an affair with her, she's like twice his age."

"She's not his type, I have to admit." Patton agrees, reluctantly.

"She's planning a big Hallowe'en fundraiser." Connie says with a shrug. "She'll probably be sorting out permission to close roads and things, you know how overboard she goes."

16

CONNIE

I'm at Adele's house bright and early. So early that Sheriff Morton is still home, playing daddy and husband before he puts on his uniform and goes off to drink coffee in secret. I try to put the thought of the two of them screaming abuse, and then getting intimate, to the back of my mind.

"Morning, Sheriff." I greet. Taylor's skittish as he flashes me a nervous smile.

"Hey, morning Connie. I was just going off for a shower, excuse me."

"No, excuse me?" Adele barks. Her hair is flyaway and her skin pale. "I thought I was going for a shower while you minded the babies."

"I can mind them." I offer.

"See, Connie can mind them." Taylor says, and he's already halfway out the room.

Adele shakes her head and smiles at me. "Men!"

"I don't mind, let him finish up and then you go do what you need to do. I'll be fine with these two cuties." I murmur as I gaze at the babies. They're both wide awake, lying on their backs on a brightly coloured activity blanket.

"It's his job, Connie. He should be doing it. He had all the time in the world a minute ago."

"He probably just remembered how much work he's got to do." I think, but I know that his sudden urgency to wash and leave would be due to my arrival. There are too many conversations he doesn't want to have in front of his wife; from his caffeine habit to the enquiries he hasn't been making into Emelza Shabley's murder. "Anyway, how are you doing? I feel like I haven't seen you much."

"I've been laying low." She says, taking a seat. She looks at me, holds my gaze for longer than is comfortable. "Ya know, we came here to escape some things. He thinks I don't know."

"Taylor does?"

"Mm-hmm." She says with a nod. She rubs at one of her eyes and suddenly looks incredibly tired. "I'd have left him if these two weren't already on the way. It's funny, the different choices you make when you're not just thinking of yourself. So I pushed him into the transfer really, said a new start would be good for us. Good for the babies."

"And it will be, I'm sure." I encourage. "This is such a great place to bring up a family."

"Oh, I see that."

"But I thought you wanted to leave?"

"What?" She asks. "No! I'm super bummed that we get here and the crime rate goes through the roof... but I don't want to go anywhere. Between us, I don't think I could handle more disruption."

"I'm not surprised." I say, but there's something about her delivery that doesn't quite convince me. She wants to leave, I can see it in her nervous energy. She's desperate to get out of here, so why is she pretending otherwise? "Look, I know things are crazy right now, but I really think this case will be solved soon."

She lets out a small moan. "I hope so. He won't talk to me about it. I know that's just him doing his job but I feel pushed out. I'm not the kind of woman who knows how to sit back and do nothing, ya know. I'm used to taking action and solving problems, and now I'm changing diapers and singing lullabies."

"Isn't it nice, though?" I ask. "The change of pace?"

"If I can stop myself feeling guilty for long enough, sure." She says. "I'll be back at work in no time. I should enjoy this time while it lasts."

"Right ladies, I'm outta here." Taylor calls from the hallway. We hear him step into his sturdy boots.

"Don't I get a kiss?" Adele calls.

He appears in the doorway, flustered. "Of course, just getting everything ready. As if I wouldn't kiss my favourite people."

He plants a kiss on her cheek, and then bends down to the floor and kisses both babies.

"Make sure you catch him." Adele calls.

"I'm going to." He says, but it's me he looks at, not her. His expression is fierce. "This case will be solved today."

And then he's gone.

"He actually said it would be solved today?" Patton asks.

I made my excuses to Adele quickly after she'd had her own shower. She didn't care. She was clean, smelling of vanilla, her hair freshly dried and straightened. If that was all the time I could give her, she was grateful for every second.

I called an emergency meeting with Patton, Sage and Atticus and they're all sat around in my attic, hanging on my every word.

"He was so determined." I say. "Like another person."

"Well, that's crazy, he's been so uninterested. What's changed?"

"Let's go and ask him." Patton says. "Something isn't right."

The police station is in darkness, although Taylor's car is in the parking lot.

The front door is unlocked though, and when there's no reply to the intercom, we let ourselves in and take the stairs up to his office.

"This place freaks me out." Patton says. "It should be a hive of activity in here, not a ghost town."

I lead the way down the corridor and see that Taylor's door is closed.

I knock lightly. No response.

"Maybe he went off on foot." I say.

"We're wasting our time on him." Sage says. "He's fooled us again. I bet he's out getting lunch."

"Okay." I say with a shrug. "Let's go."

I'm about to move away from the door when I hear a noise from within. A low, muted groan.

"Did you hear that?" I ask.

The others shake their heads.

"Well, I did." I say, and I push on the door, which opens.

The office inside is a tip, even worse than normal. Piles of papers have been tipped onto the floor, the empty coffee cups are strewn around the room, the third drawer of the filing cabinet stands open, its contents removed and rifled through.

"He's been burgled." I say with a gasp. I'm about to shout out that we need to call the police, when I realise that he is the police. If the other towns won't come out and help us with a murder, they're not going to come out for a burglary.

"Someone's gone through this place good." Patton says as he examines some of the paperwork.

"Sheriff! Sheriff, can you hear me?" Atticus calls then , and I turn around to see what he has seen; poking out from the walk-in stationery cupboard, Sheriff Morton's heavy duty boots.

I dial the ambulance as I move closer, so that by the time I see the Sheriff's lifeless form slumped into the tiny room, I'm already giving the address.

"I don't know." I say in between sobs. "There's a lot of blood. I don't know what's happened."

"Gunshot wound." Patton calls, and I repeat his words into the handset.

"Taylor? Can you hear us?" Atticus asks, his face inches away from the Sheriff's. The Sheriff's face is ashen, his eyes closed, and Atticus looks towards me and shakes his head a few moments later.

Adele answers my call on the fifteenth ring, right as I'm about to hang up. A baby screams in the background as she barks a harried hello into the line.

"Adele. I need you to get the babies ready and meet me at the hospital. It's Taylor."

She drops the phone. I hear the bang of it hitting her kitchen floor, and her own sobs ring out together with the screams of her child.

I think back to my younger days, when I was friends with a military wife. She opened up to me once about how, every single time the phone rang, her heart stopped and she expected it to be that call. The call that told her, *your husband isn't coming home*. I'd never rang her after that, not wanting to add to those times when the fear gripped her. I tried to talk about it again with her a few weeks after, but she shook her head, refused to speak of it again.

I wonder if Adele has felt the same way, that her law-enforcement husband might only be hers for a limited time, until he's taken from her. From her and their babies.

The sirens of the ambulance approach and I manage to walk, calmly, through the building so that I am in the parking lot to greet them.

"He's up here." I say, as they dash across the lot, arms full of equipment.

"Who is he?"

"Taylor Morton, he's the Sheriff. He's working a murder case right now. He told me this morning he'd be solving the case today." I explain as we make our way through the building. The paramedics dive into action when they see his slumped body, taking his pulse, checking his vitals, then quickly making the decision to transfer him onto a stretcher.

"Is the building secure? Could the perp still be present?" One paramedic asks me and a chill runs through me.

"I don't know." I admit. "It didn't occur to me."

The paramedic speaks into his radio. "We need police back up, building unsecure, perp may still be on site."

"Lift." Another paramedic says, and they lift the stretcher in perfect unison, carrying Taylor out of the room, down the stairs, and out into the ambulance.

"What shall I do?" I ask them, feeling lost and helpless. Sage, Patton and Atticus watch with me, but the paramedics can only see me.

"The police will need to talk to you. You can come to the hospital, though."

I climb into the ambulance and sit across from Taylor, cupping my head in my hands.

"He have a next of kin?" A kindly walrus of a paramedic asks me as he jots notes down on a clipboard. "That you?"

"No, no. He has a wife, Adele. I've rang her."

"She comin' here? Cos we're not waiting." He says, and right on cue, the ambulance starts up and speeds through town, sirens blaring.

"I told her to meet us at the hospital."

"Good, good." He says. "And you know him how?"

"Well, he's the Sheriff, so everyone knows him. I'm friends with his wife. They have two little babies, twins. I try to help out with them a bit."

"Childminder?"

"Oh no, just as a friend."

"Mm-hmm." The paramedic says. "You know anything about his health? Any allergies?"

"I couldn't say." I apologise. "Does it matter?"

The paramedic smiles. "We don't want to give him medicine he's allergic to, that's only gonna make things worse for him, ain't it?"

"Is he...?" I begin, and notice that I'm shaking.

"He's alive." The paramedic says, noticing my shivering body. He pulls a foil blanket from a container and opens it up, wraps it around my shoulders. "You're going into shock, keep that around you. You see what happened?"

I shake my head.

"You see anyone else in there?"

I shake my head again.

"Alrighty then, the police are gonna have some more

questions for you. They'll probably see you at the hospital. You tell 'em everything you know, okay?"

"Yes, sir." I say, pulling the foil blanket around my body tighter as I watch Taylor's lifeless body.

Adele has no babies with her, that's the thing I notice first.

She throws herself at the stretcher with such force it takes three members of hospital staff to remove her.

"Mrs Morton, please, we need to get your husband into surgery." A staffer says, pulling on her skinny arm. She bats him away with superhuman strength.

"Adele." I plead, and it's my voice she listens to, my voice that reaches her through the fog. "Come on, let them help him. Every second counts."

She steps away from the gurney, arms raised, as if she's showing them she means no harm, she's done. I lead her down the corridor and grab two empty chairs, the metal cold against our skin as we sit down. I grab her hand and hold it tight.

"Who has the babies?" I ask.

She looks at me as if she's never seen a baby in her life.

"The old witch." She says then, alarm in her voice, as if she's only just realised she's left her children.

"Violet? Violet Warren?" I ask. "Okay then. They'll be fine with her. Don't worry."

"She saw me, or heard me. She came over. And I just... I left. I left my babies." She says quietly.

"It's okay. It's okay." I soothe. "Let me give her a call."

Violet answers on the first ring, and laughs when I ask how she's doing.

"What's going on?"

"Sheriff Morton's been shot." I whisper.

"Goodness." Violet breathes into the handset.

"Are you ok with the babies?"

"Absolutely." Violet says. "Tell Mrs Morton not to worry. I'm a bit out of practice but I'll handle it!"

I smile to myself. Violet Warren wouldn't be my first choice of person to look after my babies, but she can definitely handle whatever life throws at her. She'll be fine.

"Everything's fine." I say as I return to Adele's side. "Violet loves babies."

"Oh, good." Adele says.

Look, sometimes a lie is needed, okay.

"What happened down there?" She asks me, eyes wide, as if she knows she can't handle the details but needs to hear them, anyway.

"I don't know." I say. "The office was a mess, I thought it was a burglary at first. Then I saw him..."

"Who would do this to him?" Adele asks.

"I think it was the same person who killed Emelza Shabley."

"But why?"

"He said this morning, he was going to solve the case today. I think the killer wanted to shut him up."

"Oh, wow." Adele says. She curls her legs up under her and begins to cry. "Well, they've done that."

The doctor is a stunning Arabian woman, green eyes, high cheekbones, tight smile.

"Mrs Morton?" She calls, disturbing both me and Adele from a light sleep. The world has grown dark during the time we have sat on the metal chairs, and it hurts to move from the foetal positions we've adopted as best as possible.

"Yes!" Adele says, and struggles to her feet.

"Follow me to my office?" The doctor asks, and Adele holds her arm out for me. I struggle to my feet too and take her hand in mind, and together we follow the doctor down an artificially lit, empty corridor, every step we take echoing through the medical maze that surrounds us.

The doctor's office is small, functional. The type of office that's given because her status requires one, without really being used. She sits behind her desk, where her computer and nothing else stands, and we take seats opposite her.

"I'm Dr Abaza." She says, eyes thick with mascara. "I've been overseeing the surgery for your husband. He came in this afternoon with a gunshot wound to the shoulder, the terminus of his collarbone specifically."

"The shoulder? People survive that, right? Isn't that what you aim for to not really hurt someone?" Adele asks, speaking rapidly.

"TV has a lot to answer for." Dr Abaza says. "Any gunshot wound is serious. The difficulty here, is that it's caused a pneumothorax."

"A what?" I ask.

"Collapsed lung." Dr Abaza says. "It means that the space between the chest cavity wall and the lung itself has filled with air, and a portion of the lung has collapsed. We've removed the air, and your husband's going to need a chest tube to remain in place for some days."

"I don't understand." Adele says.

"He's stable." Dr Abaza says. "Your husband is going to be okay. He's not awake yet, but you can go and sit with him for a little while."

"He's going to be okay?" I repeat, squeezing Adele's hand.

"He's a strong, fit, young man. He can recover from this. It's going to take time."

"Did the person mean to not kill him?" I ask.

Dr Abaza gazes at me, unsure how to answer this question. She's a medic, not a detective. "It's impossible to say." She answers, finally. "Some people are just bad shots."

It's hard to believe that Taylor isn't dead, as we go into his hospital room, where the only noise comes from the beeps of the machines around him. I don't know if the machines are keeping him alive, or just monitoring his vitals, and I don't want to ask.

Adele begins to cry again at the sight of him there, but she doesn't go to him. She remains near me, by the door, as if she can't quite believe it's her husband in that bed. Or as if she's scared close contact might hurt him.

"I can't believe I was moaning about him taking a shower this morning." She whispers. "And talking about his mistakes. We promised to leave that in the past, and there I am, as soon as his back's turned..."

"Adele, stop it. You love him and he loves you. Marriage is hard work. You'll get through this like you got through everything else."

"He looks so weak." She says, and it's true. "I can't believe he's survived a gunshot."

"You'll need to let him rest now." A young nurse with a kind smile says as she walks into the room. "Get some rest, and come back in the morning."

"He'll be okay until then?" Adele asks, and I sense the pull she feels, between her husband and her babies.

"He's stable, no reason to expect that to change." The nurse says.

Adele lets out a breath. "Okay. Goodnight, Tay."

I walk out before she does, giving her a moment's

privacy with her husband, but she follows me out almost instantly.

"I'll look after the babies tomorrow so you can come back." I offer, and then I notice the police officers appear. "Looks like it's time for me to give my statement. I'll see you in the morning?"

She pulls me into a huge embrace, and I manage to think mainly of her heartbreak and not how squishy I must feel to her, and then she disappears out towards the parking lot.

17

SAGE

"None of this feels right." I say, for what must be the millionth time.

Patton, Atticus and I remained at the police station after Connie went in the ambulance with Sheriff Morton. We hovered around and watched the police make cursory checks around the building before the forensic squad came in and photographed the scene and took samples, and then we watched them all disappear just in time to get back across town in time for a barbecue lunch.

We've turned the whole place upside down, and we can't make sense of it.

"We should make notes, plot out our thinking." Atticus suggests.

"Good luck finding a pen in this mess." I say.

"How can a Sheriff not have a pen?" He asks, but after fifteen minutes he realises I'm right and gives up.

"What happened overnight to make him suddenly confident he'd solve the case today?" I ask aloud.

Patton is pacing up and down the corridor, appearing in

the room every few moments before leaving and repeating the trip. "I've got it." He says suddenly.

"Yes?" Atticus asks.

"He decided to." Patton says. "He decided he was going to, that's all that happened."

"I don't understand." I say.

"Well, face it, we've been pointing him in the right direction for days and the only thing stopping him has been himself. I think, for some reason, he decided he was going to do it today."

"But why?" I ask.

"That's the bit I haven't figured out." Patton admits.

"Hold on, what about CCTV?" Atticus says. "If there's CCTV of this building, it'll show who the killer is?"

"Assuming the same person killed them both." Patton says. "They're very different attacks."

"True." Atticus says. "But worth a try."

"And, Emelza's murder was probably planned. If it was the same person, they did this in a panic because they realised Taylor knew what they'd done." I say.

"Well, how do we check the CCTV?" Atticus asks.

I groan. I've been dead too long to know how things like that work. Atticus and I both look to Patton to help.

"It should save on to the computer." He says. He sits down at the desk and moves the mouse, firing the computer up. Fortunately for us, Sheriff Morton is still logged into the system, no password needed. Patton spends a few minutes searching the computer's applications, then sighs and shakes his head. "There isn't any. I'm not surprised. It's just another expense they've cut down on."

"Well, while we're in there, is there anything else? Any files he's set up about the case?"

Patton moves the mouse around as the computer pings

and the preview of an eMail appears in the corner of the screen. "Hmm."

"What is it?" I ask.

"Let's see..." Patton says, and opens the Sheriff's eMail inbox. It's empty, apart from the message that's just arrived. "This isn't good. There's only one reason a man as messy as Morton would have a clear inbox."

"Something to hide." I say. "But who from? Nobody comes in here checking his messages?"

"They don't have to. He'll get them all on his phone too."

"He's hiding them from Adele." I say, as the realisation hits me. "Can you see what he's deleted?"

"Yep. He's not that clever." Patton says, and suddenly the screen is full of a list of thousands of deleted eMails. "Here we go."

"Ugh." I say, as I see that most of them are from women.

"Hold on." Patton says. He opens one with a subject line that says *for Adele's eyes*????????????

The message has no content but an attachment.

"Shall I open it?" Patton asks.

"You have to." I urge.

He clicks, and we all gasp at the explicit image of Sheriff Morton, still in uniform, with a naked blonde woman straddling him.

"Oh my." I say.

"He's being blackmailed." Atticus says. "Who sent him that?"

"It's an anonymous eMail." Patton says. "The address is keepquiet@mail.com, it doesn't give a name."

"Is it the woman?" I ask.

"I doubt it." Patton says. "You can clearly see her face. It wouldn't make sense for her to do it. And, look at the date on the image. It's from years ago."

"So he might not be cheating any more?" I ask, hoping for Adele's sake that he has changed his ways.

Patton shrugs. "Who knows? But why would this woman appear now and blackmail him?"

"I agree." Atticus says. "Someone's found this image and they're using it as leverage."

"Have they sent him anything else?"

Patton does a quick search. "Just one, here... it's from the same address. No content again, just a subject line. It says *7/26, remember remember.*"

"7 out of 26? What does that mean?" I ask.

"I have no idea." Patton admits. He pulls up a web browser page and types the words in, searching for cultural references that may have gone over our dead heads.

"It's just how to do percentages." Atticus says, studying the computer screen. "Hold on, 7/26, it's a date!"

"Of course." I say. "I still think of dates as 26/7."

"So, 7/26..." Patton says, and a chill runs through me.

"It's the date Emelza Shabley was killed."

We fall silent, and I glance across at the calendar that remains intact on Sheriff Morton's office wall.

"Was he reluctant to solve the case because of this?" I ask. "I don't understand what it means."

"Or was he reluctant to solve the case because he did it?" Patton asks.

"He stabbed Emelza, you mean?" I ask.

"It's a possibility."

"Then who shot him?" I ask.

"Maybe he shot himself, to throw us off the scent."

"But we weren't on the scent." I say. "Nobody had even mentioned his name as a suspect."

"Someone had." Atticus says. "The mysterious eMailer, and if he doesn't know who that person is, how could he go and arrest anyone else? Or how could he know it wasn't one of us, or Connie even?"

I shake my head. "This is getting too crazy. I don't know what to think any more. Would a person really shoot themselves?"

"People do it all the time." Patton says, which I have to imagine is an exaggeration. "As a cop, he's trained, he'll know where to aim."

"Where's the gun?" I ask.

"He had one in his holster." Patton says.

"He did?"

Patton nods. "I checked. He should always have one on him when he's on duty, so I just glanced to see if it was on him."

"Okay, so let's say Taylor killed Emelza. Why?"

"I don't have that figured out." Patton says. "Money problems, maybe? He's got two babies and a wife out of work. Maybe he went across to convince her to give him the journal, so he could sell it, and she put up a fight?"

"Hmm." I murmur, unconvinced.

"What if we're looking at this the wrong way?" Atticus says. "What if Sheriff Morton didn't kill Emelza, but whoever did knows his secrets, about his past, and used the photos to make sure he stays quiet?"

"That would explain why he didn't want to go out and arrest anyone. He can't arrest the person who did it, and if he's got any decency left in him he doesn't want to arrest an innocent person."

"You could be on to something." Patton says.

Behind us, someone begins to clap. I turn to see Wilson Bruiser, dressed as flamboyantly as always, tapping his one hand against his other arm.

"You guys are adorable!" He exclaims. "Standing around here playing detectives."

"What do you want, Bruiser?" Atticus asks.

"I just thought I'd hang with the cool kids for a while. Don't you think it's insensitive, standing around here chatting? A man died in here, for goodness sake!"

I shift a little and look down. He has a point.

"We have two murders to solve, Bruiser. Time is of the essence!" Atticus says. "Now, you, on the other hand, you're only here to cause trouble."

"I'm wounded, old pal, by your words." Bruiser says, clutching his chest as if he too has been shot. "I really had none of this disrespect when I was in charge around here."

"Oh give it up, nobody believes your lies." Patton says.

"A lot of people are dying over a book that's full of lies..." Bruiser says in a sing-song voice. He's so smug I'd like to punch him.

"Have some respect." Atticus says.

"Do we even know that Taylor's dead?" I ask.

"That's a good point. And if he isn't, he'll remember what happened. Want to confess, Bruiser?"

"Sure." Bruiser says. "I'll confess. My biggest sin by far has been loving too many beautiful women. And a few ugly ones too, if I'm telling the whole truth."

"You've never loved a woman in your life." I spit.

"Come downstairs with me and I'll show you what my love feels like." He says with a grin.

"Eww." I moan.

Patton meets my eye and then steps forward, in between me and Bruiser. "You leave her alone. She's a lady."

"Ha! You old swines are no fun. I'm out of here." He says, and off he goes.

"He's so full of rubbish." I say.

"You know, once we find his journal, we might be in a better position. Let's go back to Emelza's waggon and have a look for it." Patton says.

Emelza's waggon's been taped off now, but the tape has been in better condition. As we approach, a group of teenage boys stand around on the outside of the tape, passing a cigarette between them, daring each other to step closer.

"No way man, it's haunted!" A little ginger kid shouts, all freckles and hair so spiky it looks like he's been recently electrocuted. "You go!"

"Fine." The other boy, taller and clearly the leader, says. "Here, hold my smokes."

He passes the cigarette to the ginger kid, and then creeps under the tape, where he punches the air in celebration of his bravery.

"Go inside!" A third boy calls, and he's the muscle of the operation. He refuses the cigarette when it's offered to him and instead picks up a stone from amongst the grass and tosses it at the waggon.

"Hey!" Patton cries, and the sight of him makes all three boys scream and run into the night. "The little morons!"

"Just leave them." I urge. "They're kids."

"Kids with no respect. This is a crime scene."

"It's where a woman took her last breath, more importantly." Atticus says, giving Patton a long glare. "Never forget the human life involved in crime, Sheriff."

"Sorry." Patton says. They get along so well because Patton's quick to apologise, I think.

"Come on." I say. Surprisingly, the waggon is untouched inside. The brave gangs of kids who are visiting it at night clearly haven't found the courage yet to step inside, although that will probably change with time. "Let's look everywhere."

We spend an hour in silence trawling through every drawer and cabinet without finding the journal. Patton looks under the mattress in Emelza's bedroom, and I check under the kitchen sink. Atticus appears in the living area, looking dejected.

"It's not here." He says. "We're searching in vain."

"It's better to look and not find, than just not bother looking." Patton says. "But I think we're done. We've looked everywhere."

"How about outside?" I ask. "Maybe she hid it somewhere nearby."

"It's just grass." Patton says.

"It isn't, actually." Atticus says. "There's an old bunker not far from here."

"I've never heard about that."

"Nobody has, for years. I'd be amazed if Emelza Shabley knew of it. But gypsies pass information down from generation to generation more than the rest of us."

"Can you take us to it?" Patton asks.

"It might take a bit of trial and error, in the dark, it's been years since I've thought of the place. But, yes, I'll find it." Atticus says. He leads us out of the waggon and we follow him across the field in the dark of the night. We wander around aimlessly for a while, circling ourselves, before Atticus leads us back closer to the waggon.

"It's well hidden." Patton says.

"You'd never know it's here, unless you knew." Atticus says. "It really is the perfect hiding place. I don't know why I -"

He stops talking, and stops moving.

"What is it?" I ask.

He looks around, then bends down in the grass and begins to tap the ground. "Aha, it's here."

The door to the bunker is tiny, smaller than you'd think possible for a person to fit into, which makes it even less obviously a bunker. Atticus manages to prise it open, every pull tiring him, until finally it bursts ajar.

"I'm not going down there." I say.

"Fine, wait up here then." Patton says, already climbing down into the hole.

"Oh, alright, I'll come." I say, not wanting to stay above ground alone.

The bunker opens up into a small space, the top paneled with wood, the bottom just soil. An ancient blanket lies in one corner, long ago discarded.

"I don't like it down here." I say.

"I'll keep you safe, Sage." Patton says, and he gives my hand a squeeze. "Let's check here."

He lifts the blanket, revealing a small wooden box, which opens easily.

"We've found it." Patton says, and he holds up the treasure; a dusty, tattered old journal.

"Should we read it?" I ask.

The three of us are back in Connie's attic. Atticus has fallen asleep, tired out by his efforts to open the bunker door, but Patton sits, wide awake, by my side. There's no sign of Connie, and I try not to imagine what might have happened at the hospital; the bad news that Adele was given.

"I don't know." Patton says. "This whole crazy situation has been caused by that thing. I kind of don't want anything to do with it. It's like it's cursed."

"The only person cursing anyone around here is Violet Warren." I tease.

"Nah, she's a good witch." He says. "You can read it if you want."

I pick up the journal and open it to the front page.

"The Life and Times of Wilson Bruiser Esq; Adventurer, Discoverer, Pioneer." I read aloud.

"Well, at least we know it's the genuine article. Nobody else would describe him that way."

"Jealous?" I ask, an eyebrow raised.

"I'm not keen on a man who sends flowers to you. I guess that does make me jealous." He admits. "But, as we're just friends, I don't have any right to feel that way."

I bite my lip and swallow. If Patton Davey wants to be my friend only, he'd better get used to other people sending me flowers, because I am pretty gorgeous, if you don't already know.

"Anyway." I say, turning the page. I read the rest in silence, partly because Wilson's handwriting is atrocious, but partly because I'm sulking. How dare Patton tease me, leading me on that he wanted more than just friendship with me? How dare he!

The journal isn't as grand as the myth around it has made it out to be. It's one long letter, really. The ramblings of a vain man.

"Well." I say, when I finish. "That's that."

"What does it say?" Patton asks. His eyelids are heavy, I see. We're all ready for bed.

"Nothing at all really. It's like a diary of the women he's infatuated with from one day to the next. It makes a comment about him being the rightful mayor, which suggests to me that he wasn't actually the mayor, and that's that."

"Do you think Emelza read it?"

"I doubt it." I say.

"How underwhelming." Patton says. "To think she lost her life because of it."

I shake my head, lean back in my chair, and close my eyes. Within a moment, I'm fast asleep.

18

CONNIE

"Connie Winters?" The female officer asks as she approaches me. I stand in the hospital corridor, rooted to the spot, the anguish of the day finally hitting me. I manage to nod my head at her. "We need to speak to you today. Sorry that it's so late. Trust me, none of us want to be doing this now, but we can't let you leave without talking to you."

"Sure." I say, and I allow them to lead me into a dark room off the corridor, not unlike the doctor's office. The male officer flicks the switch and the room is illuminated by a single, glaring, overhead strip light. I squint my eyes against it. They give their names. Instantly forgettable, so I instantly forget them.

I collapse into a low chair and close my eyes for a moment, until the male officer clears his throat.

"We hear that Sheriff Morton's stable. That's, erm, great news." He says. I wonder if he's ever met Sheriff Morton. He doesn't appear particularly moved by the news that one of his professional brothers has been shot and seriously injured.

I nod again, lacking the energy for pleasantries. If they have questions, I'll answer them, but I can't give them more than that right now.

"So, um, you wanna talk us through what happened today?"

"I attended the police station and found Tay - Sheriff Morton. I called the ambulance."

"So, let me get this right?" The female says, as she scribbles notes. "You attended the station and found Sheriff Morton. Had he already been shot?"

"Yes, of course he had." I snap.

"Sorry, we just need to have all the details." She says, her cheeks flushing. She's young, still following procedure as if life is a dot-to-dot puzzle. Don't go to dot 3 until you've marked off dot 2.

"You told the dispatchers it was a gunshot wound. How did you know that?" The man asks, a little older, with a little more street smarts.

"I wasn't alone when I found him." I say, and I note the look of panic flash between the officers. "Here in Mystic Springs, we have spirits. Well, I mean, spirits are everywhere, but we can all see them here. I was with three spirits."

"Spirits?"

"Ghosts."

The female officer laughs nervously. "There's no such thing as ghosts."

"Well, there is, and I was with three of them. Do you need their names?"

They look at each other, panicked. There's no protocol for this.

"Erm, I guess." The man says finally. I provide the

names. The woman writes them down, then circles them and writes "GHOSTS?" next to the bubble. I withhold an eye roll.

"And one of them told you it was a gunshot wound, is that what you're saying?"

"Yes. Patton, he was the Sheriff before Sheriff Morton. He recognised what a gunshot wound looks like."

"You didn't?"

"I'm British." I say, although that's not necessary, my accent is still strong. "We don't have as much to do with guns as you do here."

"Was Sheriff Morton alone when you found him?"

"Yes."

"Did he say anything?"

"He wasn't conscious."

"Do you have any idea who would want to hurt him?"

"Yes." I say. "Emelza Shabley was killed recently. Sheriff Morton was very close to solving the case. I imagine whoever killed her tried to kill him, to stop him solving the case."

"Emelza...?" The woman asks, pen poised ready.

"Emelza Shabley."

"I know that name." The woman says, surprising me and the male officer both. "She comes from the Blackbottom family, doesn't she?"

I let out a small laugh. "Oh, no. The Blackbottoms founded Mystic Springs. Emelza Shabley was a gypsy."

The woman shrugs her shoulders, the point not worth fighting to her. "And she died how?"

"She was stabbed."

"Did Sheriff Morton tell you who his suspects were?"

I pause. I don't have much faith in these pair, but they're

the only chance of me getting Lovey arrested until Sheriff Morton recovers. "Yes, it was a, erm, Lovey Lovegoode."

"He was going to arrest him, was he?"

"I believe he was going to arrest him today."

"Based on?"

"Motive, opportunity, and the murder weapon belongs to him."

"Okay, that's great." The woman says, continuing to jot down everything I say. "Anything else?"

"About what?"

"About what's happened to Sheriff Morton? We'll file this report tomorrow."

"Tomorrow? Aren't you going to arrest Lovey Lovegoode tonight?" I ask, suddenly awake.

The officers look at each other again. "This is a Mystic Springs case, we can't arrest anyone."

"But our Sheriff is lying in a hospital bed. You have to do something."

"We can't." The man says, watching me with a tilted head. "But we'll make sure this is all filed."

"And a darn lot of good that's going to do!" I exclaim.

"Please, ma'am, don't get excited."

"I'm not excited! I'm infuriated! There's a murderer on the loose and you're refusing to help!"

"Well, I think we're all done here. It's been a long day and I know we all need to get some rest. Thanks for your time, Ms Winters."

And off they go, without so much as checking if I need a ride.

I do need a ride, of course, because I came in the ambulance.

I stand outside the hospital, pacing the sidewalk until my cell phone gets signal, and then dial the number.

"I thought you'd never ring." The woman's voice says, followed by a cackle. "They're done with you?"

"I'm so sorry to bother you. Could you pick me up?"

"I'll be there in 10."

Violet Warren speeds into the parking lot seven minutes later, and I try not to wonder how many speed limits she's broken to get here that fast. She's in a leopard print dressing gown that's tied at her waist and her chicken legs are bare and skinny. Old-fashioned house slippers, complete with both fur and a small heel, finish the look.

She lowers the passenger window and reaches across. "Fancy a ride, sugar?"

I let out a small laugh and the release of emotion opens the floodgates; before I know it, I'm crying as I stumble into the car.

"Oh, love, don't get upset." Violet says with a grin. The town has been wary of her for many reasons, not the least of which being that she's a witch, but despite her eccentricity and her straight-talking style, she has a good heart.

"You expected my call?"

"Well, sure." Violet says, making no attempt to pull away from the hospital. "When Adele got home without you, I figured you'd be stuck out here. I hoped you'd ring since I was up anyway. He's going to be okay?"

"It looks like it." I say, with a smile. "I don't know why I'm upset now, I think I've just been holding it all in."

"Let it out." She urges, and I nod and allow the tears to come. She gives my leg a pat and then checks her mirrors and begins to drive. The streets are deserted, illuminated by street lamps and the advertising banners on the sides of the road that promote medications I should ask my doctor for, insurance, and a nearby water park. The medication adverts still catch my eye, even after decades in the USA. It's illegal to advertise medication like that in the UK, where you trust your doctor to prescribe whatever's necessary. The US system has amused me ever since; the idea that I might go into my surgery and challenge a qualified doctor's opinion of medicine based on a 15-second ad I've seen.

I realise that the billboards have distracted me and my tears have stopped. My mind flashes back to Sheriff Morton, lying motionless in the hospital bed, or slumped bloodied in his office.

"Your mind's whirring." Violet says. "I can practically hear it."

"I'm so close to figuring it all out." I say. "I know it."

"What isn't adding up?"

"Well." I begin. "The main suspect is Lovey Lovegoode, but something about it just doesn't make sense. It seems too obvious. The weapon's his, he wanted the journal, he has no alibi."

"Innocent people don't tend to have alibis." She says with a wink. "Only a guilty person creates one."

A shiver runs over me at her words, just as we pull up outside my house.

"Thanks Violet." I say as I climb out. The air's grown chilly.

She shrugs off the thanks and speeds off down the road.

"Wake up!" I call as I run through the house towards the attic.

Atticus is sprawled across the furniture, fast asleep, but Sage is shaking the sleep away by the time I burst into the room, and Patton looks wide awake.

"How is he?" Patton asks.

"He's stable." I say. "I think he's going to be okay. Listen to me, I think we're wrong about Lovey."

"Huh?" Sage asks. "All the evidence points to him."

"Exactly." I nod. "Why would he kill someone with such a distinctive weapon, and right at the time he'd announced he'd visit her?"

"People do crazy things." Sage says with a shrug.

"It doesn't add up." I say. "I'm going over there, I want to talk to him."

"I'll come." Patton says, getting up.

"No, I need to do this on my own."

Lovey's home is in darkness, just like the rest of the street. I knock on the door lightly and wait, standing on his cramped veranda. It takes several minutes before a light switches on, and I'm glad of the cardigan I grabbed from home before setting off.

"Hello?" He calls from inside.

"It's Connie Winters, I need to talk to you."

He unlocks the door but instead of letting me in, he comes out. He wipes his eyes and takes a seat on one of the steps up to the veranda. I stand for a moment and then sit down next to him, hearing the old wood creak under our combined weight.

"Sheriff Morton was shot today." I say.

Lovey Lovegoode takes a sharp breath inward. "Is he -?"

"He's alive. He's going to be fine." I say, then fix my gaze on him. "Look, I know that you know more than you're admitting. I don't think you killed Emelza. But things are getting out of hand, you have to come forward with what you know."

Lovey sighs, links his big fleshy hands together, cracks his knuckles. "I went over to her waggon and there was nobody there. I thought I'd have a look around, for the journal. I know it was wrong but I just wanted to see it. I promise I wouldn't have taken it. I looked everywhere in the living area, and then I moved into the bedroom and realised I wasn't alone. She was already dead. I saw her, lying there, and I screamed like a girl. I panicked and I ran."

"And you didn't call the police?" I ask.

He shakes his head, the shame heavy on his shoulders. "I knew I would be such an obvious suspect. I'd said I was going to see her that night, I obviously had an interest in the journal."

"But she was killed with your dagger, Lovey."

"I didn't know that, I swear. I didn't stick around to look at the details. I saw her, I screamed, I ran."

"But you went back. You were seen, back there." I explain.

He nods. "I needed to get rid of my fingerprints."

"You know all this doesn't look good for you?"

He lets out a small, terrified laugh. "Of course I know. I've been waiting for the police to come and arrest me. I don't understand why it hasn't already happened. He even saw me that night, you know, the Sheriff?"

"What do you mean?"

"Walking back towards town, straight after finding her. I'd stopped running then because I knew that would look more suspicious! Can you believe how quick your mind starts to think in such ways?! And I passed him, on the street. He was distracted, on his phone."

"His baby was in hospital." I say.

"Makes sense." Lovey says. "He clearly had a lot on his mind. But he saw me, he waved and I waved back."

"Hold on." I say, the memory of neat purple writing in an office of chaos coming back to me. "His baby was in hospital."

"You just said that." Lovey says.

"I can't believe I didn't connect the two." I say. "Lovey, I know it wasn't you, and I'm going to help you. But I need you to help me first, okay? I've got the journal, it's at my house. Can you make sure everyone in the town knows that tomorrow?"

"Well, sure, I guess." He says, and I see him fight the urge to ask about what the journal says, how authentic it is, how valuable it may be.

"Lovey, do you know much about the Blackbottom family tree?" I ask, the police officer's words coming back to me.

"I do, as a matter of fact. Not strictly my area, but Lavinia paid me a silly amount of money a few years ago to trace her roots."

"What came up?"

"Well, she was only interested in showing the direct line between her and the original Lavinia Blackbottom. It was important to her to prove that she was the one true descendant. I did the research and then she got someone to paint a huge family tree for her. I suspect it's still hanging up in her house."

"So, it was pretty straightforward?" I ask, disappointed.

He laughs. "Not at all. Lavinia made sure it looks straightforward on paper, though. It's the most edited family tree you can imagine."

"In what way?"

"Well, the first Lavinia had two children; Lavinia and Lavonia. Lavinia had a daughter, Lavinia, and Lavonia had a son, Edward. That Lavinia gave birth to the current Lavinia, and Edward married and had a child. Now, the side of the family comprised of the Lavinias was social climbers, desperately clinging to the Blackbottom name despite marriage. The side of the family beginning with Lavonia was much more authentic, in reality, to the family's roots. They stayed true to their ancestors' way of life, which the Lavinia line was eager to move away from. The two sides quarreled something awful, before eventually denying each other's very existence. Lavinia's family tree makes no reference to them."

"But why would she want to delete them? She's always said there's no family wealth she's inherited, it's not like she'd have to share."

"Oh, no, she's doing fine thanks to the gentleman in the castle." Lovey says with a hearty laugh.

"Finian?"

Lovey nods. "She's something of an entertainment to him."

"You know him?" I ask.

"Very well." He nods. "He's one of my most frequent buyers. More money than sense, really, the prices he'll pay. His money's endless, and he likes the world to know it."

"Why does he support Lavinia? Are they in a relationship?" I ask, involuntarily thinking of the naked painting hanging above Finian's fireplace.

"Nah." Lovey says. "They're both in love with themselves too much. It's just another way for Finian to show how darn rich he is."

"Then why the need for her to hide half of her family?"

Lovey sighs. "Because the other half, the true Blackbottoms if you ask me, have kept their gypsy roots."

"So the original women *were* gypsies!" I exclaim. "I knew it!"

"Oh yes." Lovey says. "And as I said, the lineage went as follows; Lavinia having Lavonia. Lavonia marrying and having Edward. As I said, Edward married - his bride was Elsa. Their daughter was given the closest mix of their names that they could think of."

I gasp, the pieces falling into place. "Emelza!"

He nods. "Emelza Shabley."

"Lavinia knew?"

"Oh yes."

"And that's how Emelza ended up with the journal?"

"It was passed down. Lavinia the first no doubt kept it and handed it down generation by generation, and the fact that it ended up with Emelza and not our Lavinia is, I think, a clear indication of who Lavinia the first believed to be the true Blackbottoms."

"That's amazing." I say, my whole body tingling with the drama of it. One side of the family eager to continue the family's traveller traditions, the other side desperate to move as far away from them as possible. "Who says history's dull?"

Lovey smiles at me, and a light flicks on in the house behind us. I turn, to see the front door open. There, dressed in an oversized shirt that skims the top of her thighs, stands Lovell. She blushes when she sees me.

"It gets lonely in the mountains some times." She admits, with a shy smile.

"I'll leave you two to it." I say, and clamber up to my feet as quick as I can.

By the time I return home, the sun is rising and I feel wide awake, despite the fact that I've had no sleep at all. The tiredness will hit me, I know, but right now, I need to remain alert.

I tap my phone and see that I have three messages.

One from Adele saying I won't be needed to mind the babies today. Taylor's shooting is the final straw. She's packing and will leave town tomorrow with the babies.

I'd completely forgotten my rash offer to look after the babies, and I breathe a sigh of relief, although I'm troubled by her decision to leave.

The second is from Violet asking how I am.

The third is from an unknown number.

I know that you have my journal. Leave it at Emelza's waggon by noon or I will have to take matters into my own hands.

I shudder as I read the message a second, then third time.

Then I pick up the house phone and dial Adele's number. She answers instantly, and I immediately feel guilty. She must be expecting any call to be the hospital.

"It's me, sorry." I say.

Silence.

"It's Connie. Are you there, Adele?"

"Sorry." Comes the whisper of a reply. "I was just heading out to the hospital."

"Sorry, I just wanted to see if you'd heard anything overnight?"

"No." She replies. "I'll try and update you later. I've got to go."

"Sure." I say, but she's already hung up and my word is lost. I want to ask about the legal document she's signed forbidding her to take the babies without Taylor's consent. I want to ask her to stay. I want to ask a million things, but instead I listen to the dial tone and feel utterly alone.

I pad across into the kitchen and see the journal on the side, pick it up, and prepare myself for a showdown I don't feel at all ready for.

19

SAGE

*S*he's gazing at the journal, bugging out the way I used to look at the centre-page posters in my Just Seventeen magazines. Oh, the cute boy band stars were my absolute weakness in life. Those and the cheap, nasty cans of fizzy pop that the Asian man sold in the corner shop.

On the rare Saturdays that our mother remembered we got pocket money - or had enough money to keep up the commitment - I'd spent mine within twenty minutes. A quick dash down to the newsagent for my magazine, a can of pop, and maybe a 10p mix, and I was penniless again for whoever knew how long. It was worth it, though. My God, it was worth it.

So, where was I? I get the idea of a paper product causing a female to go a little weak at the knees, a little hypnotised, a little spaced out... but, let's be honest, only if the paper is showing a picture of a cute, preferably half-naked, guy.

Fusty old journals? Ain't nobody spacing out about that stuff.

So I know right away something's wrong.

The problem with Connie, though? She's a problem solver. A comforter. She mothers people like you wouldn't believe. It's like her unfertilised eggs are crying out for a baby, and we all know that's not gonna happen. So solving everyone else's problems - whether they want her to or not - is the next best thing.

That's why I hang back, just out of her line of sight, and watch her.

I could burst in and demand to know what's going on, but she'd come up with some excuse. Turn the conversation around to me, and we all know I'd only be too happy to let her.

She looks tired, which isn't surprising since she's had, like, zero sleep, and she's nursing the biggest mug of coffee the kitchen has to offer. It's a Screamin' Beans original, one from the only run of mugs Ellie ever did. They sold ridiculously well, but she couldn't be bothered with the ordering, the storing, and the complaints people came up with afterward. One woman who'd bought the espresso cup for her husband actually complained a year after because the cup had broke when her husband had dropped it on their patio. People are crazy. Connie looks after hers, and it's reserved for the days when her very survival depends on caffeine, and lots of it.

Another reason I know all is not well.

"What's going on?" Patton asks, appearing at my side. I shush him and go back to spying. The man's a total dish, but he needs to give me some space. He skulks off towards the attic, and then I feel bad, so I grab his arm and pull him back to me, a little too forcefully.

"Is that you, Sage?" Connie calls, her tone a little jumpy.

"The one and only." I say, making my grand appearance in the kitchen, Patton at my heels.

"Oh, hi Patton." Connie says.

"What's going on?" I ask, glancing at the journal in her hand. She follows my gaze and drops the journal on the counter as if it's burnt her.

"Nothing!" She says with a laugh. "Just so tired!"

"Cut it out." I say with an eye roll. "What's happened? What did Lovey say?"

She tells us everything, and I nod at her words. Of course he's innocent. I've been telling people that for ages. Of course, nobody likes to hear that, but reminding people that I'm right is one of my favourite hobbies.

"I told you so." I say.

Connie takes a deep breath and closes her eyes. "I've had a text message, I don't know who from. They want me to leave the journal at Emelza's waggon."

"What are you going to do?" I ask. "Patton, what should she do?"

Patton looks at me anxiously and then offers an apologetic smile. "I don't know. I never dealt with anything like that. Sorry."

"Seriously?" I ask, screwing my eyes up towards him.

He shrugs. "I'd say ring the cops but that's not much of an option. Ignore it?"

"That'd only bring the trouble into my home." Connie says with a sad smile. "I'm not ignoring it, I've already decided that."

"It's too dangerous to do anything else." I object, although I know that I'm wasting my breath. When Connie decides to do something, there's no changing her mind. Like when she decided to move to America and leave me behind.

Connie looks at me and I see in her eyes the same fierce determination she had as a fourteen year old when she told our mother she was getting a part-time job, and the same look she gave her each week after then when she forced a tiny wad of paper bills into the decoy biscuit barrel (that never held biscuits) towards the housekeeping.

"Okay." I say. "What can we do?"

Connie bursts into a grin. A nervous grin, I can tell, but still a grin.

"Gather everyone you can. This needs to be a group confrontation. Meet me at the waggon."

Wilson takes no convincing, of course.

I hope Patton is as persuasive as I don't need to be.

"Let's go." I say, and he holds out his hand, which I bat away. "Nice try. Come on, walk with me, just not too close."

The field surrounding Emelza Shabley's waggon is deserted, the only noise the distant hum of cars on the freeway and the occasional chirrup of a bird.

We all see her approach, teetering across the field in her heels, too darn arrogant to check whether she's being followed.

The group of us huddled inside the waggon do a collective intake of breath. This is the moment we have waited for, sitting far too close together, the proximity that's fine for an intimate relationship but awkward with everyone else. I sit wedged between Patton, who keeps his hands folded on his lap, and Wilson Bruiser, who doesn't manage to keep his own hands so still. Next to Patton sits Adele, then Connie, then Atticus, and even Finian Archbold has turned up for the fun.

Lovey Lovegoode stands hidden at the side of the

waggon's door, perspiring through a mix of the clammy air and nerves.

The woman's eyes spot the journal, lying abandoned on the back of the waggon, and she breaks out into a smile, revealing a dab of red lipstick on one of her front teeth. As she reaches for it, Connie pulls the string she's wrapped around it, tugging the journal into the waggon's slightly ajar door.

The woman gazes up, locks eyes with Connie and lets out a laugh.

"Oh, how entertaining!" She calls.

"Come in. We need to talk." Connie says, and the woman obeys, her arms crossed over her chest. As she enters the waggon, Lovey slams the door behind her and bolts it, slipping the key into his waistcoat pocket.

"You?" The woman asks, glaring up at him. "What is this? What's happening?"

"We know you killed her." Connie says, her voice firm. "Your own relative. How could you?"

"She was no relative of mine!" Lavinia roars, her voice ice and fire, as she sneers towards Lovey. "Are you spreading this ridiculous rumour?"

"It's no rumour, Lavinia. She was your blood, and you know it." Lovey says. He pushes his glasses up his nose as he speaks.

"You killed her over a journal that says nothing more than how infuriating your great-grandmother was." Wilson says with a snigger. "You could have just asked me and I'd have told you."

"Why would she pretend it said you were Mayor?" Lavinia asks, her face ashen.

Wilson shrugs. "Maybe just to annoy you, dear girl. I can see why she might be tempted."

"How dare you! Finian, have you heard this?" Lavinia exclaims, looking to her strange friend for support. Finian is, as we expected, more about a good show than any loyalty, and he purses his lips towards her in a mock pout.

"Oh, darling, you *can* be frightfully annoying." Finian admits with a shrug.

"Are we going to be much longer?" Adele whispers. "I need to get back to the twins."

Connie glances at her and shakes her head. "We're just wrapping things up. Lavinia, do you want to confess? It would make things a lot quicker."

"I have no idea what you mean!"

"You demanded the journal be left here."

"That doesn't make me a murderer!" Lavinia argues. "I want the journal, because it should never have gone to... to her. Sure, my message could be read as if it was from the murderer, I guess. Maybe I did want to scare you a little, Connie. But I couldn't ever kill someone."

"Where were you when she was killed, then?" Connie asks. "Because you weren't discussing fundraising with Sheriff Morton."

"I know I wasn't." Lavinia says. "I was..."

"Well?"

Lavinia's cheeks flush and she glances towards Finian. "I believe I was entertaining my friend in his castle that night."

Finian winks across the waggon towards her.

"Is that true?" Patton asks.

"It is indeed." Finian says as he consults a small paper day planner. He holds it up on the week of Emelza's murder - on four of the days, a small L is written and enclosed with a love heart.

"Cryptic code you've got there." Patton says with a smirk.

"I've nothing to hide." Finian says. "My discretion is only to protect the lady."

"Hold on?" I say, completely confused. "I thought this was it, we'd cracked the case. I was sure it was you, Lavinia."

Lavinia scowls at me. "I don't have to stay and put up with this. I'm a beacon of respectability in this town. How dare you all!"

"Why is Sheriff Morton pretending he was with you that night?" I ask, remembering the writing on his calendar.

"He isn't." Connie says. "He wrote it in the wrong date. You've seen the man's office. He's a good Sheriff, but he's terribly disorganised. In fact, I checked some of the other meetings he'd put on there, and two others had been written on the wrong date, too. He was in the hospital the night Emelza was killed. Apart from a short period where he got some fresh air. He left the hospital for a while, didn't he, Adele?"

Adele looks up at Connie. "I -"

"You don't know, do you?" Connie says, her tone sharp. "Because you weren't there."

"I -"

"You told me you were asleep, but that's a lie. You killed Emelza Shabley, didn't you?" Connie says, a glint of fight in her eyes. "Thank you for being a good sport, Lavinia. I knew it wasn't you. You are many, many things, Lavinia, but you're not a killer. You on the other hand, Adele. Why did you do it?"

"I - this is crazy. I'm leaving." She says and rises to her feet, where she takes a step forward. "Please move."

"No." Lovey says. "You used my dagger. You framed me!"

"It wasn't like that." Adele says.

"What was it like, then?" Connie asks. "I thought we were friends."

Adele cracks a smile then, a mean smile that betrays the poison in her heart. "I'd never be friends with someone like you. Any of you!"

"How to win friends..." Wilson mutters with a snicker.

"Oh, shut up." Adele spits. "You're such a group of small-town morons. Well done! You've finally figured it out, hey? I can't wait to get out of this awful place."

"That's why you did it." I say. "You did it so Taylor would agree to leave."

"Oh, God. You shot him so he'd really see how dangerous it is here?" Connie says with a gasp.

Adele lets out a shrill laugh. "Oh, goodness no. I shot him because he's a lying snake. And he hasn't even had the decency to die."

A chill runs through me. "Are you seriously saying you killed Emelza because you don't like Mystic Springs?"

She shrugs. "It was too easy, when the stupid girl announced the journal. Everyone wanted it. I mean, can you imagine how pathetic you all sound, going mad over an old diary of a mad man?!"

"Eh, enough of your cheek, lassie." Wilson sings in a Scottish accent, and if I didn't know that spirits can't eat or drink, I'd swear he's drunk.

"You just made it so easy." She says with a lazy roll of her shoulder. "I gave the whole mommy thing a try. Ugh. My life in New York would have been so different. Nannies, a PA, back to work after a fortnight. But this? It's a neverending hell! Feeding and changing diapers and feeding again, it's torture. Waking up - every single night? It's not the life for me."

"So, why leave? Why come here?"

"Ugh." She says. "We had no choice. It was move here,

where nobody else in the world wanted to come clearly, or no more Sheriff."

"What?" I ask. "Was Taylor in trouble?"

"You could say that." Adele says with a grimace. "Caught with his pants down one time too many."

"Then how could you go back? Even if you'd convinced Taylor to?"

"I don't need his money." Adele says with a roll of her eyes. "But I did need him with me. I take my marriage vows seriously."

"Clearly." Wilson quips.

"You can't take the babies away from him, can you?" Connie asks.

Adele shakes her head. "We signed a parenting pre-nup."

"A what?" I ask.

Adele glares at me and rolls her eyes, my lack of sophistication frustrating her even further. "It was meant to protect me. I knew he was playing away. I didn't want him to leave me for a younger model and try to take the babies."

"What changed?" Connie asks.

"I wasn't going to leave without him. And then I heard about him carrying on with that trollop -"

"Me?" Lavinia asks with a gasp.

"Her?" Finian asks at the same time.

"Secret meetings. Visits to the police station. You know what they say about small towns and everyone knowing each other's business? Oh, this place is just the gift that keeps on giving!"

"I can assure you, nothing untoward ever happened between me and the Sheriff." Lavinia says, and she opens her purse and pulls a flyer out of it.

. . .

MYSTIC SPRINGS HALLOWE'EN EXTRAVAGANZA!

The flyer declares, above a picture of a haunted house.

"We've been working on this." She announces, holding the flyer up for all to see. It's a rough drawing that a child could have created, so the crowd are somewhat under-whelmed. "Main Street's going to be closed for a grand parade! It took some planning, I can tell you!"

"And you're old enough to be his mom." Wilson sneers.

"It hasn't stopped him before." Patton murmurs.

Adele is red-faced, her eyes flitting from Wilson to Patton, before she dives across the waggon and picks up a box of matches from the side of the kitchen sink. She slides open the box and pulls out a single match, holding it at face height.

"You let me go, now." She commands, and I hear the lawyer in her. The way she can craft an argument. The authority in her tone. Her words are her weapon. How desperate she must have felt to choose real weapons instead. I try to imagine the closing speeches she must have given to Taylor, pleading with him to leave Mystic Springs.

"Adele, don't do anything silly." I coax. "Let's talk about this."

She laughs, and drags the match across the side of the box, so that a tiny flame illuminates the room.

"Adele." I urge.

"Well, I'm out of here." Wilson says with a snicker, and vanishes.

"Just let me go." She says, steely determination. Lovey unlocks the waggon door and the chill of the night air rushes into the tiny space.

"We can't do that." Connie says.

I move quickly, grabbing the journal and holding it in my hands, just as Adele tosses the match into the bedroom where she had killed Emelza.

"Everyone out!" Connie screams as the room glows amber and the flames take hold.

Lovey dashes out of the waggon, already dialling for the fire brigade. He's followed out by Finian and Lavinia, then Connie, and then Patton and Atticus.

I look across the waggon towards Adele, drop the journal, and glide, out of the waggon and into the field, the night silent apart from the crackles of the fire and the distant sirens approaching.

"Adele, just get out." Connie shouts, and I turn just in time to see Adele lurch forward, trip over the string that is wrapped around the journal, and fall flat on her front inside the waggon with a groan. She looks up as the smoke grows thick and black, and Connie moves forward, towards her.

I grab her arm and pull her to me as she begins to sob.

"We have to help her." She manages, as a terrible mix of screams, smoke and the smell of death fill the air.

20

CONNIE

hey say that a best friend is like a four-leaf clover; hard to find and lucky to have. I've been searching for a best friend for most of my life. Back when I was the geeky teenager, already carrying an extra twenty pounds and able to name every bone in the human body, you know for sure I wasn't being invited to gain entry to the cool club. I was as desperate for friendship as I was to ace my exams and reach adulthood, where I was told constantly by well-meaning teachers that I would find a place to fit in.

Where I'd be able to tell people that smoking was bad for their bones, but fizzy drinks weren't, without being called a party-pooper.

Where I'd finally find a friendship group.

Except I didn't.

I was never quite one of the group, instead always stuck out on the sidelines laughing at jokes a moment too late, playing catch up to try and work out the in-jokes. It seemed like everyone had already made their friendship groups, and I was trying to gain entry to a club that had already formed.

I was the nice, but a little too needy, woman. The one people eyed with suspicion when I tried to woo someone into falling into platonic love with me, just a little too hard. You know what desperation smells like? A *so-great-to-meet-you-let's-do-this-again-sometime* text message, responded to with silence, and followed up with an oh-so-natural *how's-Tuesday-for-you?*

Maybe that's why I was so eager to befriend Adele; new in town, friendless, overwhelmed by life, Adele. So eager to befriend her that I ignored the sharpness of her tongue, and the fact that it was me making the effort every time.

Something happened to me, when Sage restrained me and stopped me running back into that burning waggon. It was as if, suddenly, I realised I'm okay. I'm okay as I am. I don't have to beg anyone to be my friend.

And I have a best friend. Her name is Sage, and she drives me insane. But I'm also well and truly in her circle. The in jokes are our in jokes, and I probably haven't made enough effort to help other people catch up with them. She was there all along, while I was searching for someone else.

Sure, she had to die for me to appreciate the importance of a shared history, and then it was the most amazing second chance because I had her - mainly - all to myself. Just me and however many millions of spirits for her to spend her time with, and usually, she chose me.

But Sage is like one of those beautiful, rare birds. She's not meant to be locked away in a cage. She's so incredible, of course you want to clip her feathers and keep her close, but if you do, her beauty will start to fade. She'll start pecking you when you stroke her. She'll refuse to sing for you.

And one day, when you least expect it, she'll manage to escape.

Never to return.

The lunch is an array of colour, the table piled high with foods I've not bought from the supermarket in a long time. Like, years.

Four separate salads, all featuring a base of gem lettuce, are the centrepiece, and in front of them is a long plate with a selection of meats and cheese. No bread in sight. I repeat, no bread in sight. May day, may day, this is not a drill!

Yes, this is my home, and this is my food.

And today is Sage's birthday.

I know, throwing a birthday party with food for a spirit who can't eat might seem a little mean, but trust me, when she sees all of the guests I've invited, she won't care that they're eating and she isn't. She'll be far too busy being the centre of attention.

I've printed every photo of the two of us I could find and created a collage on the kitchen wall, and I stand back now and admire my handiwork. It had me up at 5am. I glance at the rows of photo after photo, and it strikes me how beautiful and carefree Sage looks in them all.

My favourite is one of her standing in her garden back in Waterfell Tweed, a young mum to two beautiful little girls. Sandy, oh so serious, gazes at the camera, squinting against the sun, while Coral strikes a pose next to her. Sage, kneeling down to child height, wears a daisy chain as a headband and enormous ahead-of-the-times sunglasses. Her smile is genuine, I know, because her nose is crinkled in delight.

I wonder at the happiness of that moment, because I remember the first time I saw the picture. Attached to an eMail, a message from home, filled with tired expletives and cries for help that I ignored. I told myself that Sage was struggling to adapt as a mum, because she was so vain and so used to being the centre of attention. I rolled my eyes at her criticisms that I wasn't there for her, wondering when she'd ever been there for me. I was in America then, high in the heady glow of romance that I'd never experienced before and haven't since, and I guess I was a little smug, to have my sister reach out and show some weakness. My sister with the perfect hair, who always knew when to laugh at jokes and exactly how loud, who had been trailed throughout her life by a gaggle of adoring boys and then men. Let her struggle, I had thought, to my eternal shame. Let her realise that life isn't all sunshine and buttercups.

She has no memory of sending that eMail. In fact, judging by the time stamp of when it was sent, in those mysterious pre-dawn hours where nothing feels quite real, I bet she'd already forgotten about it when she woke the next morning.

But I've never forgotten. I've never allowed myself to forget the one time when my sister reached out for me, and I didn't answer. How I wish, now, that I'd been there, instead of here with a no-good man. He didn't break my heart. Hearts don't break, bones do.

Hearts just feel like they're breaking.

"This looks incredible." Atticus whispers, appearing by my side. To my surprise, I find myself reaching for his hand and squeezing it, the novelty of feeling his spirit skin causing me to shudder a little as I do. "You've done our lass proud."

"I hope so." I say. I check my watch just as someone knocks on the front door.

The guests are here.

"You are kidding me!" Sage squeals, her nose crinkled, smile wide, as we jump up from behind couches, the kitchen island, and anywhere else we could find to hide behind. Patton stands behind her and scans the crowd, nodding his head in recognition at the friends who have gathered together to celebrate.

"Happy birthday!" I repeat, and my own grin feels as though it spreads across to my ears.

Sage works the room like a pro, accepting compliments from everyone she passes.

Lovey and Lovell Lovegoode stand closest to the door, and Lovell lets out a high-pitched giggle at something Sage says. Mariam and Desiree stand, holding hands, smiling at each other until Desiree meets her son's gaze. Troy rolls his eyes, faking upset at his mother's public display of affection, but to my amazement, Desiree sticks out her tongue and squeezes Mariam's hand closer.

Atticus shifts awkwardly next to me.

"Desiree's a good woman, you know." I whisper to him. "She'll take good care of Mariam."

"I know." He accepts reluctantly. "I just can't help thinking it should be me there looking after her."

"You did." I reassure him. "That's why she's grown into such a great woman."

"No way!" Sage squeals, descending into laughter. She's spotted the food. "Who catered? A rabbit?"

"Ha bloody ha." I say, pulling her in close. She smells of vanilla and sunshine, just as she always has. "I'm trying to eat better, you know that."

"Ooh dear." Troy says, glancing through towards the salad bowls. "It's like being at home. Mom makes me eat my vegetables still."

"And you'll thank me for it when you're older!" Desiree calls across the room. Everyone laughs, but nobody moves towards the food.

"I brought dessert!" Lavinia Blackbottom calls out, making a late appearance. When she says that she brought dessert, she means that Finian is following her in, and he has brought dessert. In fact, you can barely see him behind the enormous tower of cake boxes. Cheesecakes, apple pies, chocolate chip cookies, peach cobbler, an ice cream pie that people jump on so quick it's disappeared before it's began to melt, snickerdoodles, carrot cake, Boston cream pie, sugar cream pie, coconut cake and smoked almond s'mores are laid out right on the floor, because the table is full of salad, and the crowd just dive in and take their pick.

"You didn't have to." I say with an awkward smile towards Finian.

"Darling, I saw y'all at Bill's. When I saw your cart, I knew an urgent cake delivery was needed." Finian says with a wink, and he holds out a s'more towards me. "Whiskey marshmallows. You gotta try 'em."

"I guess the diet could start again tomorrow." I say with a self-conscious grin. It's difficult, being overweight and still needing to eat. Like the world is ready to judge you if anything more than a carrot cross your lips.

Finian screws up his nose. "Don't you dare. You're perfect as you are!"

I roll my eyes, unable to accept a compliment, especially from someone as thin as a streetlamp like him.

"How's Sheriff Morton?" Violet calls across the room,

her eyes somehow managing to stay open under the weight of what must be seven layers of deep purple eyeshadow.

"I rang the hospital earlier." I explain. "He's going to be okay. They might even release him this week."

"Does he know about that wife of his?"

"No." I say, and I return to the night of the fire, the surprising memory of how cold the air could be while a fire blazed before me, and the moment the lead firefighter shook his head towards me. No words were needed. That head shake told me everything I needed to know.

"What a discovery to wake up to." Violet says, lips pursed.

"If only you could cast a spell and make it all go away for him, eh?" Someone calls out.

"Oh, hush." Violet says. She does nothing to encourage the rumours that she's a witch and while I'm virtually certain that they're true, and she is, her lack of interest in the subject makes even me wonder.

"Can I get a minute with the birthday girl?" I ask after everyone else has left. Even Patton has gone, perhaps sensing that tonight, I want the last minutes of the day to be just me and my sister. Sage lies on the couch, her hair spread out around her like a lion's mane, her feet bare. She's every inch the boho princess she always wanted to be, and I couldn't love her more.

"Thank you so much." She murmurs, sleepy.

"Hey, stay awake." I say, prodding her gently. "I need to talk to you."

"So... tired." She says with a low smile.

"Trust me, you want to be awake for this. I've not given

you your gift." I say, feeling my stomach flip. I hope I've done the right thing, I think for what must be the thousandth time.

"You are my gift." She murmurs, and I'm losing her to the irresistible pull of a good night's sleep after a busy, fun day.

"I wrote to Sandy." I blurt, and her eyes are moons, wide open.

"What did you say?" She asks.

"I wrote to Sandy. And Coral... one letter, to them both. I posted it to Sandy."

"And?"

"And I told them... I told them that you're here, that I still see you, that we've found this magical place where you can be around, and be seen."

Sage sits up and swallows, and I see the emotions on her face. I see how she prepares herself, for them not believing. Because who would believe this crazy story?

Hey, your mom is dead but you can see her as a ghost!

Nobody would believe that. And so, I see her, prepare herself for their disbelief.

But then, that wouldn't be much of a birthday present, would it?

And so I pull the letter out of my pocket, where I've been nursing it for days, wondering when the perfect moment might be. I give the letter a little squeeze, and then pass it to her, and watch her debate whether she wants to read this or not.

"It's Coral's writing." She says with a gasp, the concrete reality of holding her daughter's handwriting bringing her to tears. "I can't -"

"You can." I say, and although she tries to hand the letter back to me, I push it back towards her. "Read it."

And she does. Silently.

I know it word for word, I've read it so many times.

Dear Aunty Connie,

Thank you for your letter, which we were very surprised to receive.

We are glad to hear that you're well. We are too.

We are confused by everything you've told us, and that's why it has taken so long for us to reply. We didn't know what to think, or say, about the things you are claiming.

We don't believe in ghosts - you should know that. Of course, we feel mum with us sometimes, but doesn't everyone who has ever lost someone? It doesn't mean that she is really there. We don't believe that she is really there, or anywhere, since she died.

However, we are curious. We'll admit that.

And, we miss our mum terribly. If what you're saying is a joke, or a trick, it's incredibly cruel. But, if there's even a tiny chance that you're telling the truth, I guess we have to give it a go. We would do anything to spend one last day with our mum.

So, I guess we're saying yes.

We will come.

We will come and see you.

And we are trying not to get our hopes up, but we really, really, hope to see mum.

With our best wishes,

Sandy and Coral

"They're coming?" She asks, meeting my gaze and blinking at me. I nod.

"I suggested they come for Hallowe'en."

"That's just a few weeks away." She says, eyes wide.

"I know." I say with a grin. "Happy birthday, Sage."

She shakes her head and stares off into the distance, then lies back down on the couch and, clutching the letter to her chest, slips into a deep, happy, sleep.

THE END

BONUS CONTENT

Would you like to see how The Secrets of Mystic Springs began in my mind?

If so, I'd like to share with you my author notes and my initial, handwritten plan for this book.

You'll get to see just how much the characters took control once I started writing!

To get these exclusive bonuses, give your details here:

http://www.monamarple.com/ms2

THE CURSE OF MYSTIC SPRINGS

Roll up, roll up, it's time for a show.
Onwards to Mystic Springs we go.
The spooks are out for All Hallow's Eve
Many will come, but not all will leave.

Prepare for Hallowe'en in Mystic Springs, where it's clear that more than ghosts wander the town.

Lavinia Blackbottom has planned a spectacular celebration but all does not go to plan.

At the end of the festivities, a curse is placed over Mystic Springs and a man is found dead.

With magic controlling the town, it's time for one reluctant witch to accept her powers and save Mystic Springs.

Pre-order your copy of The Curse of Mystic Springs now at mybook.to/TCOMS

ABOUT THE AUTHOR

Mona Marple is a lover of all things bookish. That's a word, right?

She is happiest when she's either curled up reading an excellent book, or hammering away at her keyboard trying to write one.

She's been creating characters and worlds since she was a child, and never forgets the magic of being able to connect with people through her writing.

If you've enjoyed this book, Mona would love to connect with you.

facebook.com/monamarpleauthor

twitter.com/monamarple

instagram.com/monamarple

amazon.com/author/monamarple

pinterest.com/monamarpleauthor

bookbub.com/authors/mona-marple

goodreads.com/monamarple

ALSO BY MONA MARPLE

Mona Marple writes cozy mystery and paranormal cozy mystery books, with a new release available most months.

You can check out all of Mona's books by visiting:

author.to/MonaMarple

Made in the USA
Middletown, DE
31 July 2019